MW00895292

# THE GIFTED OF
# SISCERLY

*William Buckel*

iUniverse, Inc.
Bloomington

# The Gifted of Siscerly

Copyright © 2011 William Buckel

All rights reserved. No part of this book may be used or reproduced by
any means, graphic, electronic, or mechanical, including photocopying,
recording, taping or by any information storage retrieval system
without the written permission of the publisher except in the case
of brief quotations embodied in critical articles and reviews.

This is a work of fiction. All of the characters, names, incidents,
organizations, and dialogue in this novel are either the products
of the author's imagination or are used fictitiously.

iUniverse books may be ordered through booksellers or by contacting:

iUniverse
1663 Liberty Drive
Bloomington, IN 47403
www.iuniverse.com
1-800-Authors (1-800-288-4677)

Because of the dynamic nature of the Internet, any Web addresses or
links contained in this book may have changed since publication and
may no longer be valid. The views expressed in this work are solely those
of the author and do not necessarily reflect the views of the publisher,
and the publisher hereby disclaims any responsibility for them.

Any people depicted in stock imagery provided by Thinkstock are models,
and such images are being used for illustrative purposes only.

Certain stock imagery © Thinkstock.

ISBN: 978-1-4502-8504-9 (pbk)
ISBN: 978-1-4502-8505-6 (ebk)

Printed in the United States of America

iUniverse rev. date: 1/12/2011

For My Mother.

# THE GIFTED OF SISCERLY I
## *Trouble at Cambells Cross*

LIGHTNING WAS NEVER so bright or thunder so loud as when Kamahl the war wizard fought. His bolts and rays of white hot light obliterated all in its path. The hooves of thousands of charging horses sounded through the valley as Kamahl's serpent soldiers raced toward the defending troops.

Nikita Princess of Tyhton rode at the head of her army opposing the wizard. Thousands of mounted soldiers charged her way. Hundreds died at the raising of her hands. It was as though a typhoon swept them from the backs of their horses and an invisible herd of wild beasts trampled them to death. Their armour was crushed and their lances broken at a mere wave from the hands of the sorceress.

The wizard's tempered lightning cut into her forces as well; hundreds lay smouldering behind her.

Nikita looked upon the four sapphire storage rings, her power source. The two on her left hand were drained, glowing no more. The two on her right hand fading. She had to back out. Outnumbered more than two to one she ordered a retreat.

The great horde would crush her tiny force.

Nikita guarded as they ran, her blonde silky hair blowing in the wind. She wore clothes white as snow and rode a horse so bright it gleamed in the sun. She defied them to come after her; the Princess of Death awaited them.

The Tyhtons raced across the fields and over the bridge to the south side of the Mensys River. Nikita's archers and foot soldiers lined the banks in support of their fleeing comrades.

Nikita ordered the bridge guarded and burned if the enemy tried to cross. The river was deep and wide; she could hold the invaders here for a time. Kamahl the war wizard and his soldiers had taken three countries before attacking Tyhton. Nikita abandoned the northern part of her land to save the southern half. She hung her head in sadness having to leave the villagers in the north to the whims of the wizard; he would enslave them all. Nikita put Amie a sorceress in charge then rode to her castle at Siscerly to plan her defence.

It would be a fight to the death between the most sinister of men and the most dangerous woman in the world.

Not far from the battle and unaware of the upcoming danger Jensen filled her basket with wild flowers. Squirrels scolded her as she went, birds sang in the trees. The sun was bright and climbing high in the sky. A gentle breeze blew wisps of hair into her face. She hummed a tune her mother had taught her; a silly melody but catching none the less. She stopped at the roll of distant thunder and looked to the skies; there was not a cloud to be seen. The sound grew ever louder as she scanned the valley below.

Hundreds of soldiers mounted on horses were charging toward her tiny village. She dropped her basket and ran down hill, her mind numb, tears flowing. Faster and faster she went until she fell. While catching her breath she looked on: the hamlet was already overrun, villagers rounded up like cattle then driven inland. Where were they taking them?

It's not fair she thought as tears streaked down her cheeks.

Jensen's village, her family, her friends, were on the north side of the river. More invading horse soldiers flooded in by the minute. They forced the Tyhton troops south. Some soldiers unable to get to the crossing ripped off their armour and dropped their weapons so they could swim to the southern shore. Some didn't make it; some drowned.

Two armies now faced each other on opposite banks. Thousands of soldiers with all manner of weapons clattered along the shores. Her little village was filled with men, wagons, and horses. Her family and friends had been taken away. She had to do something.

Jensen stood then gasped as near her sitting upon a horse was an enemy soldier, a smile on his face. The soldier dismounted and threw his armour to the ground as he walked her way; his shirt came off next. Jensen started to run but a hand caught her in mid flight pulling her to the ground. The man was on top of her reeking of sweat, his pungent fish breath choking her. His smile widened exposing dirt coated teeth.

With both hands Jensen pushed up against his chest and squeaked, "Please let me be."

Tension built within Jensen, fear gave way to anger then rage. She felt a surge rush through her body to her hands, and then to his chest. The soldier's body jolted as though being punched. All emotion flowed from her to him. Jensen was drained. The soldier's stare turned solemn, his eyes blank. He appeared to be in a trance. The soldier stood then walked toward his shirt putting it on then his breastplate as well. Jensen watched astonished at the sight.

Maybe the man had children of his own; maybe conscience would not allow him to proceed. Maybe the man had heart and would help her. Jensen was only a girl and could do nothing for her family and the others but the sorceress could. She had to get across the river to the castle at Siscerly and see her. The sorceress would help; she had to help, so many lives were at stake.

Jensen felt like running but there was nowhere to run. She felt like screaming and crying but what good would it do. She had to stay calm and convince the sorceress to give aid. Maybe the soldier would help.

"I need to get across the river, can you help?" asked Jensen.

The soldier mounted his horse and walked it her way then reached down and scooped her onto his steed. She held on as if her life lay in the balance; he rode into the valley toward the bridge. Near the crossing soldiers stood in neat rows waiting for an order to attack.

The bridge was guarded by a hundred men on both sides, the only way across the river for miles. The soldier rode over the crossing without stop, not challenged by his men as they stood aside. Jensen thought him to be a man of some rank and definitely a kind one.

On the other side he faced the enemy their arrows nocked and bowstrings pulled back. The soldier showed no emotion as he gently lowered her to the ground. He turned and rode back to his side of the war untouched by soldiers on either end. Jensen's hands were high in the air as he crossed; a plea not to fire on the man who had just helped her to freedom.

Jensen saw a woman making her way through the troops toward her. It was odd to see a woman walking amongst all these men. The woman was about her mother's age and dressed like a peasant but had the look of someone in charge. Her long brown hair shone in the morning light and on her face was a look of dignity. The woman looked at Jensen long and hard then spoke.

"What is your name girl?" she asked.

"Jensen Taggart and yours please?"

"Amie. Why did that man bring you across?" asked Amie.

"Because I asked him to. I think he is a good man."

"It was Kago. Commander of the enemy troops. Not a nice man," said Amie.

"I don't know why then. I only just met him."

"Where are you going?" asked Amie.

"To Siscerly to the castle. I have to see the Sorceress on an urgent matter. Many lives are at stake," said Jensen.

"I am going back myself. You may come with me," said Amie.

Jensen was given a horse to ride and managed although she'd never ridden before. Jensen didn't know why this luxury was bestowed upon her as she was only a peasant from Cambells Cross. Twice in one day she had the pleasure of meeting two very nice people and would soon see the sorceress. Jensen would explain the needs of her people and knew that help would soon be on the way. She smiled at Amie who granted her a gentle look in return.

Jensen's horse crested a hill. She was not prepared for what lay ahead. Jensen looked in awe at the sight before her. In the valley below rose stone walls, high and long. A gentle mist obscured the view; not everything could be seen. Towering buildings of all shapes and sizes stood high over the barriers below. Exposed were the road and a bridge leading to two large wooden gates. She followed Amie into the valley to the castle unable to take her eyes off the sight, not even wanting to take the time to blink. They crossed a stone bridge spanning a stream not far from castle.

Close to the walls Jensen looked high pushing her head back in discomfort to see the top. There were tiny shapes of men looking over the edge toward her. The gates creaked open as they approached and Amie nodded to the guards on either side. They saluted her and Jensen was sure she saw fear in their eyes.

A cobblestone yard waited as they entered, the sounds of their horses echoed from the walls. A huge fountain stretched high before her, water falling to a large basin below. Birds of all kinds flew overhead from great white swans to sparrows landing on the statues throughout the square. Pigeons cooed from every ledge and finches flittered through the bushes.

Jensen's eyes scanned the ramparts alive with soldiers moving back and forth. She followed Amie through winding streets to a tall stone building so high the top was hidden in the mist. Two giant towers on either side stretched to half its height. From them came the sound of music known throughout the realm as the bells of Siscerly.

Jensen felt like a trespasser in another world. She knew that this was the palace where the sorceress lived; stories told of such a place but Jensen had thought them exaggerations.

Fables they were not, as no words known to her could describe the sight before her.

They stopped in front of the highest building and soldiers took the reins then led their horses to a stable below. Jensen followed Amie into the building. Amie led the way to a large hall near the entrance; marble benches lined all four walls. She was told to wait patiently as the Sorceress was a busy woman.

# THE GIFTED OF SISCERLY II
## *The Sorceress*

JENSEN LOOKED AT OTHER people waiting, some eating, some fidgeting and looking about. Those eating reminded her that she had no food since breakfast and it was early evening at least. Jensen hoped they were not all here to see Nikita as it would mean a long wait for her, she being last in line.

The one thing all the others had in common; they all wore their Sunday best. Jensen looked down on her old worn out dress covered with grass stains and dirt. It was the dress she wore to do her chores. She a had new one for market day and Sunday picnics. Jensen could look equal to any of them if she'd had the chance to prepare.

Jensen thought about what she would be doing if she were at home; thought about the times before the soldiers came. She would be finished with supper and had the dishes cleaned. Her brothers would tease her all night. They always started when they got home from work in the fields. Her oldest brother Colby was due to wed a maiden in a village not far away to the south. His wife to be would still be safe on this side of the river. The youngest by a year, Jarrod was the worst, the hardest on her. Their whole lives they had fought; how she wished they were fighting now.

Amie came her way not dressed as a peasant but in a white robe with red trim known by all to be the dress of the sorceresses. On a golden chain around her neck was a pendant with a dragon etched upon it, the sign of the Mother of the Realm. Amie was the Mother guardian and protector to all in the land. Some called her the Legend of Tyhton, Jensen having grown up listening to stories told of her.

Jensen dropped to her knees afraid to look up, her forehead touching the ground. A gentle hand raised her back into the bench but she kept her head turned afraid to look into Amie's eyes. It was said that the direct look of a sorceress would render a person mad at best. Jensen was not about to put that tale to a test today. There was too much at stake, the lives of all those at Cambells Cross.

Amie said, "Nikita will not have time to see you today. You will have to find lodging for the night."

Jensen rose to her feet, head low, "I have no money for food or lodging."

"Oh, I'm sorry I should have known, please follow me," said Amie.

They left the palace and crossed a square to a building several floors high.

"These are the chambers of the Sisters of the Sun. You will be safe here. There is an empty room at the very top of the stairs, on the left," said Amie.

"Where can I find something to eat?"

"Oh, I'm sorry; it has been a tiring day for me. Follow me."

They went to a market across the street; a place of dreams for Jensen, not like anything she'd ever seen. At Cambells Cross they'd had one store that sold all. Here under a huge canopy supported by beams and trusses, rows of shops and tables stood separated by wide aisles. Coats and dresses of all colours and styles hung from cords spanning the upright beams. Shoes, boots and sandals were stacked on tables and in cupboards. There were fruit stands and vegetable counters everywhere. Amie stood in front of one that specialized in bread and dried meats.

Amie put some of the bread and salted beef in a cloth bag and gave it to Jensen. She now had at least one possession, a bag full of food.

"Here take these coins. You may need them," said Amie.

Jensen stared at the coins; a fortune given to her. Amie took Jensen's face in both hands and looked straight into her wide eyes.

"It's not true. A sorceress cannot turn a person mad with just a look. Now put the coins in your pocket and eat. Come back to the palace at dawn."

In the dwindling evening light Jensen walked the roads toward the front gate. At the sound of hooves upon the cobblestones she ran to the side away from the street. Well out of the way she backed up even farther. They were Lancers riding out to war on horses larger than she had ever seen; men in armour with weapons hanging from their side. They galloped by with their face shields down and looked like mounted ghosts; their lances pointing high in the air, a terrible threat to behold. Who could defeat men such as these in battle? Who would even stand to fight them thought Jensen.

Chewing on bread she strolled closer to the gate and

watched men returning from daily battle make their way slowly up the street. Their armour was covered in blood and some rode head down, one man even fell to the ground, his armour clanging as he rolled. The soldiers helped the injured man to his feet and carried him behind the others.

Jensen walked back to the Sister's chambers easy to find the way guided by the palace lights. A man walked from one torch to another lighting them as he went, the torches hissing on being lit. She climbed to the top of the stairs and entered her room weary from a day she would never forget. There was a large bed within and a wash basin set on a small table. She checked under the bed fearing someone in hiding then felt foolish when there was nothing there. Jensen washed her face and lay in bed thinking about her plight. She felt so lonely tears ran from her eyes. She had to keep her mind on the task ahead. Convince the princess that help was needed.

Jensen had just turned sixteen and the world lay ahead. Men noticed she was alive but reluctant to come close. Her mother told her it was her red hair and hazel eyes, all signs of a witch. No one in her family had red hair, only her. Which was further proof some said that she was possessed. Jensen had been hexed before her life had even begun. A cruel joke played upon her by the Gods.

Miranda was also on Jensen's mind as she lay and wondered what was happening to her. Her best friend since six years old, they were both the same age. Miranda was a dark haired beauty and the soldiers would want her. The boys in the village used to chase her as she teased all but would commit to none. Miranda told Jensen she dreamt of a knight and not a farm boy. Her friend dreamt of a man in white armour riding a white horse to come and take her away.

11

Maybe Miranda got what she wished for. Jensen decided not to worry about her in any case. She had beauty beyond compare and would have soldiers fighting over her, killing each other with her as the prize. Miranda had a knack for doing things to the hearts of men and would survive anywhere.

Jensen woke in the morning to the sound of horses galloping down the street. She had been told to attend the palace at first light and knew not what time of the day it was. She threw her bag over her shoulder and ran downstairs then across the square to the palace. Jensen walked unopposed by the guards into the large hall and sat. There were a dozen people already waiting so she cursed herself for sleeping in. She chewed on the last of her bread and waited. One by one the other people went in then left, half the day went by.

Amie came to her holding out a hand, "Come Nikita will see you now."

Jensen was taken up many flights of stairs into Nikita's stateroom. Inside was a table with a woman writing on parchment, no one else in the room save Amie. The woman's blonde hair glowed in the sunlight that penetrated the windows beside her desk. Jensen stood near but the woman did not look up. An eternity passed as Jensen rubbed her hands against the sides of her dress.

"What do you want of me Jensen Taggart?" said the sorceress without looking up. Her voice was full and made Jensen jump.

"We need your help. Cambells Cross has been overrun and the people taken somewhere. I don't know where," said Jensen.

The Princess of Tyhton finally looked up, the most beautiful woman Jensen had ever seen. Jensen felt her penetrating eyes probe her soul, look close and long as though searching for something.

"You will do as everyone else in this land. You will fight. You will have to free your own people. I am busy with a war," said the Princess of Tyhton. Each word was pronounced loud and with clarity.

"Fight with what? I am only a girl. I have nothing to fight with," said Jensen, tears running from her eyes.

"You are an enchantress, a woman with the power to control men, so use that power like other gifted," said the Princess then started writing again.

"Me an enchantress? I don't even know what that is. I have no control over men. What are you talking about?" cried Jensen.

Amie stepped forward and spoke, "I saw you make Kago the Butcher ride you across the bridge and set you gently on the other side. Had it not been for the magic within you would have been used then enslaved like other women he fancied."

"I still don't understand. What am I supposed to do?" said Jensen.

"According to the old books anger is the key. Rage will build and bring forth the surge of power that dissolves a man's will. It is also written that as you grow stronger under severe anger your touch can be lethal.

"Normally your touch will soften a man and he will do as you say. Every woman has power over a man to a certain degree, some more than others. Once in a million or maybe less one is born with a thousand times more control over the opposite sex than others. The old books call a woman with that gift an enchantress. You are the first in a thousand years.

"There is no defence for man against the power of an

enchantress. Once touched by her he would forever be under her spell," said Amie.

"How do you know what I am?" asked Jensen.

"Everyone has an aura or ambient light that emanates from within. Other gifted can see this light. We can see what is in the heart and souls of people. Nikita and I both see you have the distinct violet glow of an enchantress as described by the old scrolls. You also have the mark described in the Book of Locke. An eagle on your right arm," said Amie.

"Mother says it's a birthmark, that's all. I touched boys at the village and nothing happened with them," said Jensen.

"The gift would not show itself until well after you have become a woman. It also requires great emotions on your part to make the gift work. Had you stayed you would have married the first man you fancied, had children and never known what you were. Fate brought you to us and now you know," said Amie.

The princess raised her head and spoke.

"I have need of you Jensen Taggart. My first Knight, Corel Blue, is missing. If you find him ask him to help your people. After that I need him here."

"How do I find him?" asked Jensen.

"Start at Sharks Way. He knows a witch named Katie who lives there. Amie will give you clothes suitable for your journey and point you on your way," said the Princess then started writing again.

Jensen walked out of the room and down the stairs, Amie at her side.

"She's very harsh and blunt isn't she? She doesn't care about my family or the villagers," said Jensen.

"Nikita has a lot on her mind. She's only five years older

than you. She's seen a lot in a short time. Her father was tortured to death by the wizard, Kamahl. He caught him returning from their country residence," said Amie.

"They say a Wizard is more powerful than a Sorceress," said Jensen.

"It's true but Nikita has many talents, as she was born of a Wizard and a Sorceress. Niki is the first to stop him. Let's pray for her and do your best to find Corel. He's a womanizer and a scoundrel but no one can plan battles as he. Don't even try to use your power on that man, the outcome would be unpredictable. " said Amie.

"Maybe he ran out?"

"Him, oh no, he knows no fear that one and if he did would rather die than admit to it. Men like him don't run," said Amie.

"Wonder what's happened to him then?"

"He's probably under some witch's spell," said Amie.

"My power won't work with women though. Will it?" said Jensen.

"That's right, it won't, but it will work with men. Get them to do the dirty work for you. Know this Jensen that you are immune to the power of other gifted. Your power is of this earth and is pure, untainted, so has precedence over the conjured spells of the less gifted. But above all remember that no matter how powerful your foe you are immune to magic. Your life however can be ended by a simple arrow the same as anyone else," said Amie.

Jensen felt both powerful and weak after that. She realized that she was still mortal despite her gift.

They went to the market again where Amie purchased travelling clothes for Jensen and stocked her for a journey.

"Here's a purse full of gold and silver coins for you and a horse you already have," said Amie.

"She's a little bit slow and looks sleepy."

"That's Biscuit. That little mare is one of the best in the stable. The horse gets bored just walking though. You might want to ease her into a run occasionally that's when she comes alive," said Amie.

"Well alright, but you know what I'm scared. I still don't believe I have any power and I'll be out there on my own," said Jensen.

"I was eighteen when I went out on my own discovering my powers as I went. I know it's not easy. It's a hard life for one and all but we have to find our own way and most of us do," said Amie.

"I'll get some sleep and start out at first light. Good night Amie," said Jensen.

Jensen returned to her room and looked at her new riding clothes. Amie had given her cotton under garments and a wool shirt. The trousers were also made of cotton with leather patched in places of wear. Amie also gave her a dagger that was infused with magic and a light crystal that would light her way out of the dark.

Before anything else she would find a bathtub and have her first bath in three days. Jensen would not go to sleep dirty again. She found a tub and the sisters helped her fill it with water both hot and cold. They even scrubbed her back like her mother used to do. She went to bed and was soon asleep.

Next morning Jensen woke with the sun then dressed and ran to the stable for her mount. It was only the second time in her life she'd ridden a horse. She rode Biscuit toward the castle gate determined to find the first Knight.

Amie watched Jensen leave the castle grounds and was joined by Nikita.

"Well, what do you think?" asked Nikita.

"I think she'll be all right. Lots of spirit in her, I sense it don't you?" said Amie.

"Yes but I still think she needs help. Why didn't you go with her a ways?" asked Nikita.

"She has power we could use on our side against Kamahl but of no use to us if she's too afraid to stand on her own. The best person to help her right now is Katie. That witch is a sucker for anyone in need. As soon as she sees that little girl all alone, Katie will help her."

# THE GIFTED OF SISCERLY III
## *The Witch*

JENSEN RODE THROUGH THE front gate and over the bridge leaving the safety of the castle behind. She crested the valley peak and looked back, the morning mist again covering parts of the walls and top of the palace. She reluctantly rode Biscuit down the road into the unknown, the horse moving ahead with no more enthusiasm than her. Their ride to Sharks Way took them over gentle rolling hills and through the woods. She met no one only animals of the forest. Chipmunks came out of their holes, squeaked at her then ran. Pigeons flew from the road and deer raced into the forest as she came.

Jensen assessed her journey so far. She never thought she would have a horse of her own or wear clothes like these. It was a new world and she was lost in emotions running both hot and cold. Hot when thinking of the riches that had come her way: a horse, the clothes, and a purse full of coins. She felt cold when thinking of her family's plight. How was she to save her kin?

Jensen was out in the world on her own and not a clue

about life. Her father used to tell her that in this world people died of stupidity. The trick is not to be one. At sixteen how was she supposed to know what was smart? She needed someone to guide her; Amie shouldn't have let her go alone. Jensen asked herself what was she doing out here by herself? Tears started to flow. Panic set in; her breathing went wild and her heartbeat did as well.

One step at a time her mother used to say, one step at a time. Do not look too far ahead or you'll trip over something at your feet, her mother used to go on. All right, we'll find the witch Katie and take it from there. She petted Biscuit on the neck, not alone after all. That's our one and only worry now to find Katie; simple as that. This road leads to her and the knight needed to save the people at Cambells Cross.

What if the witch wasn't friendly though? She'd heard most of them were not. Most of them were mean or so stories went; most of them were evil and dark. Her power if she had any at all would not work with women so if the witch was sinister or menacing she would be lost. A witch woman could turn someone into a toad. But then her power would save her from another's spell. At least she hoped it would. What if the old books were wrong?

Jensen heard the sound of horses thundering her way, the same noise the invaders made at Cambells Cross. She walked Biscuit deep into the woods and watched as the soldiers raced by. They were Lancers running to or away from something. Later that day she found the reason for their flight; a large clearing to her left was full of dead soldiers. Biscuit was on her toes hard to hold, the smell of blood was strong in the air. The men's bodies lay scattered, their horses gone. It looked as though every single one had been struck by lightning; they were both mutilated and burned.

Hundreds lay dead.

She wanted run but maybe there was someone who needed help. What could a sixteen year old woman do? She would tell what happened at Sharks Way, there were men there that could help.

Jensen stared at the orange light forming in the skies above the field. It was like the sun only in the wrong position for this time of day. It grew in size and intensity then flashed sending a lightning bolt which severed the tree at her side. The tree split in two, one half coming her way. She jumped to get clear. Biscuit ran. Another bolt hit her in the chest knocking her to the ground. Jensen was certain death was coming her way. She searched for blood but found none. What was her gift of touch supposed to do for her against a power such as this?

She was a joke.

No wizard was in sight only that orange globe but she knew it had to be him. Who else could it be? Jensen rose to her feet and was immediately struck down by another lightning bolt sending her tumbling. As she struggled to her feet fighting for breath another bolt came. Her right hand rose to stop it. It hit like a giant fist knocking her arm backward but did nothing more.

Jensen looked to the orange ball, "You can't kill me like the others, I have a gift."

She said it to bolster courage more than anything else.

The orange ball hovered left to right as though lost then raced away out of sight. Jensen's body tingled then started to buzz like her arms were falling asleep. She walked toward the road then heard the distinct sound of a man moaning.

She turned grasping the hilt of her dagger then saw a soldier struggling to his feet. Smoke came from the uniform under his armour. Jensen unclasped the hot chest plate and tossed it aside, then did likewise with his helmet. She took the dagger from her side and cut the smouldering vest from his body. His wounds were not severe. He would only suffer bruises and burns.

Jensen left the man at the side of the road and looked for Biscuit. The mare was not far and appeared to be searching for her as well. The little mare was lost and frightened; they both were. Jensen helped the young man into the saddle and led the horse down the road. She had survived the Wizard's wrath; her gift had protected her from his blows. She was in no hurry to meet him again and would avoid him if she could.

Her gift was no joke.

Late that evening, the sun half hidden behind the hills, Jensen walked Biscuit to the edge of Sharks Way. The little village less than a day from the castle was a port to the sea and lands beyond. Jensen led Biscuit down the main street looking left and right. She'd never been to a coastal village, a place where sailors came and went. She'd heard stories about the men of the sea, their drinking and what they did to women young and old. She couldn't see any; they weren't waiting for women on the edge of town.

Jensen looked the length of the street, seeing few people. No sound except the barking of a dog and the eerie creak of a windmill. As she neared the centre of the village she heard the bellowing of men and music in the distance. Those were the sailors she'd heard about.

Cautiously Jensen approached a store and tied Biscuit outside. She checked the young soldier drooping across the saddle and made sure he was still alive. He seemed to be as far as she could tell.

Jensen had to find help or all she'd done would be for nothing. She would go inside and ask. There was but a single soul inside, a big man wearing a white apron and pushing a broom.

"Excuse me sir but is there anyone who could help a wounded soldier outside?"

"The only one who can heal is the witch Katie. At this time of day she'll be at the inn at the end of town," said the storekeeper.

"Thank you."

"No problem."

Jensen held the reins tight as she approached the inn, the bellowing of men louder the closer she came. Sailors came to the porch and looked at her, bottles in hand. She wanted to turn around and go back as they stared at her and grinned.

"You looking for a man young lady? It looks like the one you got couldn't handle you. Maybe I can," said a sailor.

They all laughed.

"He's hurt can't you see. I'm looking for the witch Katie."

"She'll be inside. You know where I am if you need someone tonight," said the sailor.

They all laughed again.

Jensen tied Biscuit to a pole beside a water barrel so that the horse could drink. The men still stared and laughed at times. Her fear was replaced by anger. Who did they think they were? She came in friendship and looked for no trouble; they gave her nothing but ridicule and scorn.

Jensen entered the inn to the sound of men talking and

laughing; cries of victory and defeat as they arm wrestled at a table before her. On her entry all sounds ceased, their eyes focused on her. A man grabbed her pants and refused to let go. He laughed and looked to the others thinking it was a joke. Jensen was in a rage as she stared at him then grabbed his hairy arm. A surge ran through her body to the sailor. It felt as though she was going to explode until the rush entered him.

"Let go and never touch me again."

The man's grip released as he stared at her, a blank expression on his face.

"Now get out," said Jensen.

The man left in a trance. The others must have sensed she was gifted so sat in silence looking down avoiding her eyes. It was the first real test of her power so far and it worked as Amie said it would.

Jensen looked for a witch yet found none; none that fit her perception of what a witch woman would be. She walked to the innkeeper and asked for Katie. He pointed to a red head sitting at a table with a big mug of ale. Beside her was a muscular man with blonde hair drinking as well. The woman was about twice Jensen's age with a full figure build. Jensen's first thought as she looked at Katie was a hope that someday she would look like her. Her tight blue robe was tied at her waist by what appeared to be a dead snake. The witch was laughing and looked friendly enough. Caution though she thought. Remember what father said about people dying of stupidity.

Jensen approached Katie, smiled then spoke.

"I need your help with an injured man outside."

"Can it wait till morning?" asked Katie returning the smile.

"I don't think so. He has been struck by the Wizard's lightning," said Jensen.

"All right. Let's go tend to your friend," said Katie.

"He's not my friend. I just came upon him near the road. He's just outside. I hope it's not too late. There are hundreds of others dead in the field."

Jensen felt nervous as the witch stared at her long and hard then broke into a gentle smile.

"You're gifted aren't you? I can feel something, something I've never felt in a person before."

"At the castle they say I'm an enchantress. They say I have power over men."

"Is that what happened with that sailor. I thought I was going to have to come over and help."

"You'd help me?"

"Of course. We women have to stick together," said Katie.

This witch was as friendly as they came. Jensen and Katie took Biscuit to a cabin at the end of town. Katie helped the young man inside all by herself. The witch was strong having no problem at all handling his weight.

"He has been struck by Wizard's lightning alright. Your gift probably saved his life," said Katie.

"How can that be?"

"I don't know but he should be dead by now if not for that. The Wizard's lightning is a tempered flash meant to kill. Did the Wizard fire at you?" asked Katie.

"Yes three times, he finally left."

"He probably made your power stronger with his energy. He won't make that mistake again. He'll be careful of what he sends your way." said Katie.

"Will the soldier be alright?"

"Yes, he'll live."

Katie returned to the inn, she said the night was still young. Jensen lay near the hearth thinking about her long day. Her mind was a blur with all that happened; it didn't seem real. She'd lived more in one day on the road than her whole life at Cambells Cross. She soon fell asleep telling herself that it had all been a dream.

# THE GIFTED OF SISCERLY IV
## *Assassins*

WHEN JENSEN WOKE THE young man was sitting, Katie stroking the bruises on his chest, a smile on her face. This witch liked men too much thought Jensen.

"What is your name soldier?" asked Jensen.

"Shaun."

"Katie, I'm told you know Corel Blue, have you seen him?" asked Jensen.

"No not lately, about a week ago he passed by, never know where that one will be," said Katie.

"I was with him yesterday," said Shaun.

"Where is he?"

"He said he was going to Kettle Peak. He rode off alone. It was the last I saw of him," said Shaun.

"Why would he go there?" asked Jensen.

"I don't know, he didn't say anything, just left," said Shaun.

"Maybe to see Kenji," said Katie.

"Who's Kenji?"

"She's an old Sorceress who lives there. Wants nothing to do with people," said Katie.

"So why would he go there? I have to find him. I need him to save my family. Kamahl's soldiers have taken my parents and Nikita said to ask Corel for help," said Jensen.

"One thing I do know, there's nothing else up there that a knight would be interested in," said Katie.

"Shaun and I will go find him and ask," said Jensen.

"Oh no, I'm going north away from this. If you had seen what I'd seen you would go too," said Shaun.

"Shaun, if Jensen says you're going then you're going. Don't fight it. I'll get you some clothes and help you change," said Katie.

"Katie, I have to ask. Why do you wear a snake around your waist?" asked Jensen.

"It's a swamp Adder. It bit me. It was the closest I ever came to dying. Right after it bit me I thought I was a goner so bit it. It died, I didn't. I had Sammy a friend turn it into a belt. Reminds me never to give up," said Katie.

Jensen thought about that and didn't know whether to believe her or not. It was the strangest story she'd ever heard but then everything the last few days had been strange. What was so strange about biting a snake? Right now she would bite one herself.

"Where can I get a horse for Shaun?" asked Jensen.

"At the stables. We'll get him one when I get mine. I'm going too. It's been a long time since I've seen Kenji. Too long. Besides you'll need me to get in," said Katie.

Jensen watched as Katie helped Shaun change; she saw how much it excited the young man. Embarrassed she turned her head and stared out of the window. This village was so much like her own, people busy trying to make a living, half their labour going to the tax collector at the end of the month. More now she thought as it probably cost a fortune to finance this war; a war no one wanted but Kamahl. What makes some men think they have a right to take from others; take lives without remorse. Nothing was ever enough to satisfy those heartless souls.

Jensen had finished step one in finding Katie and set out on step two. The witch was certainly friendly and it looked as though she was going to help. She could use it too. How would she find Kettle Peak on her own? This man loving witch was really something. She was certainly bewitching Shaun. He'd better watch it as that's what witches do. The witch woman made Jensen smile.

Two read heads walked through town to the stables. People scurried out of their way. They bought a horse for the young soldier and within minutes were on their way to the hills beyond. Jensen looked at Shaun dressed in the clothes of a peasant, and thought him to be a handsome young man. He was tall but not too tall, just right and that long dark hair fit well around his slender face.

Shaun was not a man yet as far as Jensen was concerned. He was trying to run out on his obligation which made him seem more like a boy than she wished him to be. Jensen could not dream of leaving her parents as slaves to Kamahl and would risk all to set them free. Both her brothers were strong and would last until she found help. She worried about her parents though. Rumour had it that the commander in charge of the mines started each day with a beheading. The slowest labourer was killed for all to see, and then the rest put to work.

No one wanted to be the worst except those seeking to escape the agonies of life.

"What's the name of your horse Katie?" asked Jensen.

"Snowflake."

"Snowflake? He's brown."

"So what? I call him Snowflake because he was born in a winter storm. He came into this world in three feet of snow, with an icy wind that almost froze him where he lay. I covered his body with mine and he's alive today, so be it, Snowflake it is," said Katie.

Jensen didn't know whether to believe that or not. This witch came up with one strange story after another, nothing seemed real. Nothing in the last few days seemed real.

"What are you going to call your horse Shaun?" asked Jensen.

"I don't name horses, it's a silly thing to do," said Shaun.

"What? You have to name your horse, it's courtesy as he carries your weight. Who else would do that for you but a horse?" said Jensen.

"Well all right I'll call him Idiot then because I would not carry him," said Shaun.

Jensen liked this man less from day to day. He was arrogant and self centered. The kind of person she avoided at Cambells Cross. He'd been hurt but so had others. They didn't take it out on the world. Katie seemed to like him for some reason though so she would keep her mouth shut.

Jensen felt a presence and looked about, then saw a man on horseback coming from the forest. Two others rode out of the woods to join the first. Jensen caught Katie and tapped her shoulder wanting her to look back. Katie smiled and nodded without turning her head. She knew they were there all along.

Shaun finally looked over his shoulder and wanted to run. Katie grabbed his reins and pulled him to a walk.

"Let them make the first move. Don't let them run you into a trap," said Katie.

"Do you think there's more ahead?" asked Jensen.

"Maybe. But why run if they're no threat. They're just men and what's wrong with men?" said Katie.

"You're man hungry Katie."

"Ever since the snake bite," said Katie with a smile.

Jensen kept Biscuit at a walk, the day dragged on but eventually night was upon them. They camped and gathered wood for a fire. Jensen brought dead grass so the sticks could easily be set aflame. Katie swept her hand over the dry wood and flames sprang forth. Wow thought Jensen. She'd never seen that before. Katie piled more and more wood on the fire until it was bright and high. Jensen wondered what she was trying to accomplish as the flames were too high for cooking.

"Come, join us. Don't stand out in the cold," said Katie as though to herself.

The three men following them came forth swords in hand looking at Shaun as he was the only one armed.

"Come now. It's a night for firelight and love. Come on big guy, come here," said Katie.

Jensen watched as Katie walked toward the biggest and meanest looking of the three. She pulled her belt from her waist and playfully wrapped it around the man's neck kissing him on the lips in doing so. She let go of the belt and turned her back on him starting to walk away. As she did the snake belt turned into a real snake, wrapping around his neck and biting the startled man in the face, then dropped to the ground and slithered away. Katie walked away from camp into the dark bush followed by another of the three. Shaun ran to her aid.

Jensen didn't think Katie needed help but looking at the man approaching her knew that she did. His broadsword slashed the air in front of her so she pulled her dagger, tiny in comparison to his weapon.

"Oh no," said Jensen. She would swear but her mother had warned Jensen not to use words like that. Her mother had probably never confronted a man with a sword only holding a little dagger. What good was the magic of her touch in times such as these? She couldn't get near him. She remembered what Katie had done so followed her lead.

"Come on big boy. It's a night for love," said Jensen.

The man held his weapon and refused to meet her half way. Jensen dropped her dagger and smiled but his eyes were still full of hate as his friend lay groaning, dying of snakebite. She ducked a sword slash and prayed for help, it was all she could do. Out of desperation she grabbed her dagger lying on the ground. He struck downward and she parried his blow with the dagger expecting to be cut in two. His sword shattered like glass on contact with her little weapon. She looked at him astonished by what had transpired then rose to her feet and grabbed his arm. She felt her power surge and flow.

"Did Kamahl send you?" asked Jensen.

"Yes he did," said the man.

"I never want to see you again. Understood?" said Jensen.

The man ran to the woods, not a look back. Katie and Shaun came out of the darkness talking to each other not acknowledging her presence. The man following Katie was gone. Katie searched and searched then finally pulled the snake

31

from under a bush and as she grasped it the snake turned into a belt that she tied around her narrow waist. Katie took rations from her horse and announced that dinner would soon be served.

Jensen looked around not sure whether to believe her senses as to what had occurred. Shaun seemed at peace in Katie's hands, sitting near her, living off her strength. Katie had taken this day in stride more upset at having to leave the bar last night than what had transpired today. Jensen shook her head wondering what kind of company she was in. She wondered what Kenji would be like, another sorceress she had yet to meet.

The world away from Cambells Cross was a strange place.

# The Gifted of Siscerly V
## *The Seer*

Presela felt the bark of a tree as high as she could. The world beyond her touch was foreign to her. Presela was blind, had been since birth. She lived in a poor village and was born to poor folk. Her father had been killed in a war not long after she was born, she couldn't remember him at all. Her mother cleaned a castle from dawn until dusk bringing home two copper coins a day, barely enough to feed and house both.

Presela spent most of her childhood feeling, touching, exploring the world with her hands. She formed images in her mind based on what her fingers saw. There were gaps though; she felt and knew what a tree trunk was but what was above remained a mystery to her. The world she knew was as high as she could reach and the rest a blank.

Her mother Shayla told her she had become a woman one day when she was thirteen years old.

A week later she started to see things but only in her mind; her eyes were still dead.

Presela said she saw the sun, the moon, and the stars then

described them to her mother. Shayla said it was impossible for her to know. Presela saw people long since dead and things that had yet to happen. She saw great seas, deserts of sand, jungles, and forests dense and vast. Her mother called it a miracle but told her to say nothing as some might believe her to be a witch, and witches were sometimes burned.

Presela found a kitten half starved in the castle one day: took it to her room, fed it and nursed it. She grew to love that cat she called Cromby and took him everywhere. Then one day after the cat was grown she could see.

Presela saw through Cromby's eyes.

Presela could even see herself when Cromby looked her way. She saw her white dead eyes, they frightened her. She wondered if they frightened others as well.

Shayla grew tense when Presela told her the news and started to weep. She called Presela a Seer and told her how lucky she was to be gifted in such a way. Shayla still worried and told her to say nothing as trouble may follow. There was nothing to be gained if other folk knew.

One day the village baker's son was lost and she could stay silent no more. She knew where he was or could see him anyway. He clung to a bucket hanging from a rope up to his waist in water and surrounded by large stones. Presela told the villagers what she saw. They pulled him from the well behind the bakery shop, everyone amazed with Presela that day. They were to have free baked goods for as long as they lived.

News spread and people came wanting to know of loved ones lost. Some she saw and some not, some were forever gone. Either way a silver or gold coin was given for her gift or things that she saw.

One day Kamahl the wizard came and invited her to visit

his castle. It was an honour to attend so she and her mother went.

Years later at twenty-two she was still there as an advisor to Kamahl attending his court daily. She would tell him things he needed to know, sometimes he was pleased and sometimes not. He could be a harsh man when he wanted to be expecting perfection from all.

Then one day her world changed and things would never be the same. Kamahl came to her more upset than she had ever seen. He showed her images on a magic wall of a young woman younger than she, only a girl. He tried to kill her with lightning bolts but failed and needed to know more about her he'd said. So she was helping a killer and her life would never be the same in doing so.

Presela saw the young woman and her plight; her parents and brothers taken to Kamahl's mines. She saw her save the life of a young soldier and take him to a witch. She could say nothing about Jensen as Kamahl wanted that young woman dead. Presela could not help him do so. Presela was to meet with him and tell him all of what she saw and knew.

"I can tell you nothing as I know her to be the victim. You have no right to end her life. I know what you are and I serve no devil," said Presela.

"I'm going to have your mother locked in her room and a guard posted at her door. If you don't tell me what I want to know then I'll take her to the dungeon where we will both go and watch her tortured. I've treated you like an equal at court and you repay me this way. You will do as told. Do you understand?" said Kamahl.

Presela held Cromby tight as her cat trembled. She could not let her mother die but did not want to see Jensen dead either so would tell him only a little; only where she was and no more. She hoped the young woman could look after herself as she'd done before.

"I asked if you understood," shouted Kamahl.

"Yes, I do."

"Well then tell me."

"Her name is Jensen and from what I've seen has the power within to control men. They call her an enchantress at the castle it seems. She's at Sharks Way. It's all I know, her name and where she is," said Presela with a sob.

Presela watched him as she spoke and what she'd said upset him even more. He sat wringing his hands and staring into space; she saw it all through Cromby's eyes.

Presela saw fear in Kamahl. He was afraid of Jensen.

"Get out and come back when you have more news," shouted Kamahl.

She left but knew she would have to escape as sooner or later the madman she now saw would kill her mother. She could not help him murder, that much she knew. Presela had never hurt a soul and things that she told him could result in another's death. She would have to run but how?

# THE GIFTED OF SISCERLY VI
## *The Underworld*

THE ROAD TO THE mountains quickly turned into a trail forcing Jensen to ride behind Katie and Shaun. She looked over her shoulder often, afraid more assassins were on their way. She wondered if the Wizard was watching her now or if he even could. She had no idea the extent of his power but remembered the field full of dead soldiers and knew he was not to be taken lightly. Katie had told her the trip would take a day and a half then she would meet Kenji and hopefully Corel. The first Knight was the only hope to free her parents and the other inhabitants of Cambells Cross.

The forest slowly changed from hardwood to softwood with spruce and pine dominating the scene. A thick cloud of mist blocked the horizon before them. Jensen watched as Katie stopped and looked at the fog before her seeming unsure of what her next step would be. It was the first time she had seen the woman hesitate and knew there was trouble ahead. Jensen rode through the thick grass to her side.

"What is it Katie?"

"It's not a good place but we have to cross. There's no way around. It's a gate to the underworld, realm of the dead," said Katie.

"Let's go back," said Shaun but neither acknowledged him. Jensen saw him drop back twenty paces probably hoping they would follow.

"Have you crossed it before?" asked Jensen.

"Many times, but I sense the forces trying to get out are stronger than the forces now keeping them in. Kamahl is probably weakening the barrier," said Katie in a tone and manner more serious than Jensen had seen her to date.

"What good would that do him?"

"If he rules the dead then he rules an army that no one could oppose," said Katie.

"What if they take control of him instead?"

"That's what we think would happen. The end of life but he is willing to take a chance," said Katie.

"Can anyone stop him?"

"I don't know. Maybe Kenji," said Katie.

"Is she powerful enough to stop a Wizard?"

"I don't know that either. She is as old as time itself I am told. She guards her secrets well and keeps to herself sharing with no one," said Katie.

"Let's go through this, we have no choice."

"I know. Follow my exact trail," said Katie.

Jensen walked Biscuit through the wall of mist behind Katie not knowing what to expect within the white shroud. It was very dense, so dense in fact she could not see Katie's horse only two paces ahead. Jensen stiffened with apprehension squinting to see before her, afraid to look to either side or back. The fog quickly ended as they broke through to the other side.

Jensen took a deep breath and held it as she looked about not believing what lay before her. They had just come from a world of green and brown, of life, sunshine, and sound. They had come from a land of animals, birds, and insects, of blue skies, and warmth.

This place was dead.

The sun was hidden behind an iron sky in a world filled with many shades of grey. Jensen doubted the sun ever shone in this place. There was no green or brown to be seen as even the water was a murky grey with white film scattered throughout. The horizon disappeared in the mist behind dead stands of leafless trees. Their rotted limbs made them look like ghosts reaching for the sky. There was not a bird to be seen or heard: no animals, no frogs croaking, no crickets chirped, no identifiable life to be seen. There were no bulrushes: no grass grew on shore, not even green algae floated in the water. Jensen listened for the sounds of flies usually associated with things no longer alive but even those were absent here. Jensen breathed deep taking in the pungent odour of something long dead. It was as though life was not allowed here at all.

Biscuit walked ears back, nervous, searching for a reason to run. Katie was in the lead, their horses to their knees in dirty water. Jensen looked toward the grey skeletons of trees around her and wondered how they ever came to be. She gasped as bubbles rose from the swamp to her left. Her eyes fixed on the sight, trembling she watched the bog churn. A torrent of water gushed into the air then rained down exposing a huge skeleton. It was the skeleton of a snake, high as a tree and moved as though alive. Its four fangs gleamed as it opened its mouth wide. The horses as of one mind rose to their hind legs plunging all three riders into the murky swamp. Their mounts ran to shore. Jensen jumped to her feet standing in water almost waist high. She watched Katie unwrap the snake belt and taking it in both hands it transformed into a golden broadsword.

"Touch it Jensen," yelled Katie.

"Are you crazy?"

The snake skeleton swooped down at Katie each of the four fangs half her height. She swung the sword cutting a piece from the top off a tooth. The snake lunged and Katie swung again. Over and over the snake skeleton tried to grab hold of Katie but she was able to fend it off, growing weaker by the second.

"Grab the damn thing," yelled Katie.

Katie was in trouble. Jensen needed to help so did as Katie requested trusting the witch with her life. She drew her dagger and jumped to the snake's head as it lunged toward Katie. It quickly snapped Jensen in its jaws and raised her high in the air. She drove the blade into the bone above. It burned but had no devastating affect on the revived dead beast. She grabbed a tooth for support and felt her power surge from her hands to the tooth. The tooth shattered. She grabbed the other and it too blew to shreds at her touch. The snake skeleton tossed her back into the swamp. Jensen jumped to her feet and ran towards it intent on doing more harm. The snake sank from whence it came, back into the dirty water, short its bottom teeth.

It was gone.

"What happened? Why did it break when I touched it?" asked Jensen.

Katie gulped for air leaning on her sword, her chest heaving madly, "I heard once that the touch of and enchantress could do that."

"Why?"

"Ask Kenji, she told me. I don't know," said Katie still fighting for breath.

"Oh no, where's Shaun?"

"On shore. He beat the horses back," said Katie.

"He's a coward."

"Now now, he's young, give him time," said Katie.

Katie leaning on her sword pulled it from the water and held it to her waist where it quickly turned into a snake belt once more.

"Were you telling the truth about the snake biting you?" asked Jensen.

"Jensen, would I lie to you?" said Katie shaking her head.

"You look like crap Katie," said Jensen.

Shaun seeing the way clear, no trouble ahead rode his horse toward the two redheads their mounts in tow.

Jensen followed Katie through the rest of the swamp, nothing else wanting to test them this day. She passed through the misty wall on the other side, the world returning to normal as quickly as it had changed before.

Jensen looked high to the peaks beyond hidden until now by the fog. They followed the trail taking them through a mountain pass between two white capped peaks. Spruce and pine trees were not as dense and shorter in length at the higher altitudes. Birds flittered about as a herd of deer grazed in a meadow not far away. The sound of wolves howling in the distance reminded her not all the world was at peace.

It was early summer but the air was chilly and getting

colder as the day wore on. Jensen stopped beside Katie who until now rode only in her robe. It was just knee length so when she sat astride her horse exposed her thighs. Shaun's eyes had been glued to that sight most of the trip. Jensen watched the young man eyeing Katie as she slipped into pants, pulling her robe high as she did. Katie smiled his way as she slowly pulled them into place. Oh, she loved to tease the young man thought Jensen. They all put on their winter coats and took advantage of the last hours of light to climb higher into the pass.

Jensen being a farm girl fell into her role from the first night they camped. She unsaddled the horses, gathered fire wood, and cooked. A town girl, Katie spread her blanket on the grass and rubbed her feet, Shaun looking on. Katie's only contribution was starting the fire. She would pass her hand over the branches and they ignited into flames. Jensen was content to have Katie's company and cared not about equal contribution.

A camp fire was a necessity that night as the icy breath of winter refused to give way to spring. The snow that fell melted on contact but was heavy nonetheless. The horses were hobbled and ate freely from the lush grass. Their ears shot back and their heads rose whenever a wolf howled in the distance.

"How far to Kenji's place?" asked Jensen.

"Tomorrow will take us there, past midday," said Katie.

"You said she was old as time. What does a woman old as time look like?" asked Shaun.

"You'd be surprised. I don't know how old she really is. She talked of Nikita's father when he was but a boy," said Katie.

"That would make her over a hundred," said Shaun.

"Too old for you then, you won't even have to check her out, right Shaun?" said Jensen.

"Now now Jensen leave the boy alone," said Katie.

Jensen eyes met hers and for the first time since meeting, Katie gave her a warm motherly smile. A smile that said please leave the boy alone. She looked at Shaun and also smiled his way but shifted her eyes and lips while doing so making the young man shuffle in discomfort. Oh, he wouldn't sleep much tonight praying for Katie to come his way. Jensen only shook her head. Katie sure loved to tease him alright.

"So, do you have a boyfriend back at Cambells Cross?" asked Katie.

"Two actually," said Jensen lying to Katie. What did she expect to hear; that guys avoided her.

"What are their names?" asked Katie.

"John and Joe," said Jensen immediately thinking it was stupid to come up with two names like that.

"Which one are you going to marry when all this is over?" asked Katie.

"Neither, I'm going to be like you and stay single. Just have friends, you know men friends," said Jensen knowing she didn't have a clue as to what she was talking about.

"It's a lonely life all alone," said Katie.

"So why live it that way. The way you look you have a choice," said Jensen.

"Things happen. Life doesn't always unfold the way you want it to. A wrong choice can leave you adrift for a long time," said Katie.

"There you see, that's why I won't choose," said Jensen.

"Hah, life will choose for you then. Sooner or later someone will come along you can't walk away from. And he'll break your heart just because he can," said Katie.

"What was his name?" said Jensen.

"Me? Oh no, witches don't fall in love. We bewitch men that's all. Don't you know that," said Katie.

Jensen could tell by the look and tone that it was not the question to ask. Katie loved somebody and might tell her someday but Jensen would never push.

"Let's get some sleep, morning will soon be here," said Katie.

Jensen tried to sleep but found none.

"Katie."

"Yes."

"How will I know if someone loves me or it's just my power making him care?" asked Jensen.

"I don't know how to answers that. I've never been and enchantress myself. I think you'll know; something will be different from the others. It's always like that, something's different."

Jensen listened to Katie and felt that the witch knew what love was all about.

"Go to sleep Jensen. You think too much," moaned Katie.

Morning found them high in the mountain pass between two snow covered peaks, rocky hills on either side. Trees were few and short, most no taller than a man, deer and birds were also in short supply. Eagles replaced hawks gliding in the heavens looking for unsuspecting game.

Jensen spent more time than the others looking back and to the sky for signs of the Wizard or his henchmen. She spotted an orange ball above then looked to her right to make sure the sun was still there. It was. There were two suns in the sky. No way.

"Oh no," said Jensen.

"What?" asked Shaun.

"Straight ahead, up there," said Jensen.

Jensen saw Shaun freeze, his horse's reins pulled tight. She knew he would remember that sight from the field where he was wounded. All she could do was brace for impact. The disk flared and lightning fired into a snow covered mountain ridge at their left. Again and again the lightning struck until the snow rolled down the mountain side. It was coming her way and nothing she could do would change that. There was nowhere to run and little time to do it in. Jensen braced for death, her life would end at only sixteen, having taunted a power greater than she could comprehend.

Something strange happened before Jensen's eyes. The snow slowed down, now only creeping its way downhill.

"Run, Run!" yelled Katie.

Shaun's eyes were still fixed on the orange ball, a death grip on his reins. Jensen slapped him hard in the back of the head then in his face, over and over until he followed Katie. Biscuit galloped and had the pass been wider would have overtaken the other two. She was embarrassed for thinking her an old nag at the beginning of the trip. Jensen looked to her left, the snow still creeping as though time had slowed but only on that mountainside. Katie stopped, Jensen moved to her side, Shaun was still on the run. They were clear of the avalanche. The snow had actually halted and lay on the side of the mountain not having touched the pass.

"Thanks Kenji!" shouted Katie.

"Was that her slowing the snow?" asked Jensen.

"Yup, you just met Kenji," said Katie.

# THE GIFTED OF SISCERLY VII
## *Kenji*

THEY FOLLOWED KATIE UP the mountainside. The orange ball disappeared having failed once again. Jensen knew that at this rate it was only a matter of time until her luck ran out. The wizard was dispatching stronger magic her way day by day; first men then a monster and now an avalanche. She hoped Kenji would have some answers and if not her seventeenth birthday would not take place.

Katie turned her horse into the rock face and waved her hand causing an entrance to appear before her. Jensen followed then Shaun did the same. They were entering a large cavern, jagged icicles hung from the ceiling. The rocks closed over the entrance sealing it at the wave of Katie's hand. She put all their mounts inside a pen and watered the animals with Shaun's help.

Jensen studied the cavern; it looked natural, jagged walls and ceilings like a cave she had seen near Cambells Cross. She followed Katie down a passageway that looked man made, the walls were smooth as glass. Higher and higher they went, up stairs and along corridors, lit by hissing torches. There were many such corridors and stairways, a maze that led to who knows where. Jensen knew that Katie had been here before as she did not hesitate and took each turn as it came, sometimes choosing one of four directions.

Katie stopped before a doorway and waited in silence. Then as though given a cue that only she could hear opened the door and moved forward. Jensen entered behind Katie then stopped in amazement at what lay ahead.

There was a room as large as the meeting hall at Cambells Cross. The walls were of polished rock and cut straight, not the work of nature or man, the work of magic. The ceiling was high and round wheels hung from above holding a hundred candles each. Tapestries of nature scenes were everywhere from mountains to forests and animals of every kind, some she had never set eyes on. A thick carpet covered the floor and lavish furniture set upon it. Golden ornaments set on tabletops and shelves. Figurines of animals made of gold, silver, and wood were scattered in careful arrangements throughout. At the very end of the room stood a chair of silver, gold, and covered with leather. In front of the chair stood a young woman, at a distance the most beautiful woman Jensen had ever seen.

Jensen walked through the huge room filled with gold and silver yet could not take her eyes off the young woman standing in front of the chair. Katie hugged the woman for a time, head on her shoulder the way family does.

"It's been a long time," said Katie.

"Almost a year now, I miss your visits," said Kenji.

Jensen looked into the face of the young woman and guessed her to be no more than twenty. Her skin was white, not pale, just the colour and look of milk. Her hair was long and black, her eyes large, dark brown in color. A look of peace and tranquility covered her face. Her voice was hardly more than a whisper yet audible as a shout. She was the most beautiful woman Jensen had ever seen. The woman Katie said was old as time.

"Jensen wishes to speak with you," said Katie.

"You have questions for me Jensen?" asked Kenji.

"Have you seen the knight Corel Blue?"

"Yes he passed two days ago on his way to people of Cameria."

"Where is that?"

"Through the mountains. Katie can show you the way."

"Can you help me please? My family is held captive by soldiers of the wizard. I need to free them."

"You are the enchantress, you need no ones help."

"The wizard is trying to kill me and almost succeeded at the base of your mountain."

"He fears you. You're the only one who can kill him."

"What? How?"

"Your touch. The touch of the enchantress is a touch of pure love, pure good. The wizard is a product of pure evil. In opening the doors to the underworld he is as they are, dead, living in this realm but more dead than alive, no feelings, no soul," said Kenji.

"Is that why my touch shattered a beast from the underworld?"

"Yes, if it came from the world of the dead it is pure evil in this world and your touch will destroy it."

"How many like me are there?"

"Only one walks the earth at a time. Good has always defeated evil and hopefully always will as if evil wins and rules it would be the end of mankind. Where would man be if mothers ceased to love their children, if men and women no longer loved each other?"

"Can you not come forth and destroy the wizard?"

"I cannot and will not interfere in the affairs of man. I will however help you, the way one helps another in need. I offer you a gift, not one of magic but of friendship. Wearing this amulet will hide you from Kamahl. It is all I can do. Hide you from someone wishing to do you harm," said Kenji.

"I thank you."

"Enough talk of the world and magic. I desire and need the company of two women. Can you do that Jensen? Be company to an old woman," said Kenji.

"Yes I can. What do you put on your skin to make it look so soft?" asked Jensen.

"Oh, I have a mixture of plants I'll tell you about."

Three women talked as women do, Shaun asleep the whole time not by choice but due to a snap of Kenji's fingers. His stare annoyed her. They had an evening meal especially prepared for them by Kenji in her kitchen. She loved to cook and had many thousands of years of experience.

"You may return any time you wish Jensen. The wave of your hand will open the front entrance," said Kenji.

"How do I find my way down the corridors?"

"As Katie, if you are welcome the way will appear before you, if not you will be forever lost."

After breakfast the three left not sure who was going where.

"I've got to find Corel. He's the only one who can help free my family," said Jensen.

"Let's go back Katie," said Shaun.

"I think I'll tag along with Jensen. It's been a while since I've seen the Camerians," said Katie.

"Is there any place you haven't been?" asked Jensen.

"Cambells Cross."

"Why would Corel go to Cameria?" asked Jensen.

"It's next in line for conquest if Tyhton falls to the Wizard."

"Why are you helping me? I mean I need it and all, well thanks I mean."

"Just tagging along," said Katie.

Shaun followed, probably afraid to return on his own. He was dead weight as far as Jensen was concerned but Katie wanted him around so let the matter lie. She would be lost so far without Katie; would have died at the hands of three assassins sent by the wizard the second day of her journey. She didn't know why Katie was risking her life to help but was glad the witch did. Her company alone was worth the gold Jensen carried in the purse given her by Amie. Jensen felt at ease after her visit to Kenji. She wore the amulet and knew the Wizard could not track her. Jensen also knew that she could kill him with her touch and his magic could not directly put and end to her. It was just a matter of getting close enough to Kamahl to touch him; simple as that, yah, simple.

Presela knew she could receive information but had no idea how it happened; it was just there whether she wanted it or not. After seeing Kamahl's images of Jensen through Cromby's eyes she could see the girl at Sharks Way. All she needed was something to make contact; a piece of clothing or a picture. She'd found people from accurate drawings of their faces or paintings if the image was close enough, thanks to Cromby's keen sight. If nothing of a person's things could be found and no drawing existed then she was unable to help.

Presela could also scan a location; a place she knew existed like her old house in the village. She could see who was there now. She had been to Siscerly a few times and had touched the palace of the Princess so knew where it was. She knew the name Nikita and Amie; who they were and where they lived. She'd seen Amie enter the palace once when she was at the market across the street so knew her by sight, or at least by Cromby's sight.

Presela had been working on sending information by way of her mind. If successful she'd be able to communicate with anyone she could read. It was a harder process than receiving but if she could tell what a person was thinking then could probably send thoughts as well. That is exactly what Presela did with Cromby; read his mind and thoughts so she could see what he saw and heard. Now all she had to do was send her thoughts to Cromby. She could tell the cat where to go whether left or right, forward or back. Her plan was to send Cromby ahead, a scout of sorts so that she and her mother could escape. Knowing what lay ahead gave her a chance. It was a simple plan and all she had.

It was time for her daily council to Kamahl so she put Cromby into her dress pocket and went.

"I can no longer see Jensen. After your attack they knew you were aware of them. A sorceress named Kenji gave her an amulet that has blocked me. I'm sorry but I am not to blame, I can't see her anymore."

"Yes, yes, I knew that sorceress would be trouble someday. You know, all I'm trying to do is make this a better more orderly world. There are those who thrive on anarchy and despair, I'm not one. I want to rid the world of those that profit from the misery of others. In order to do that I have to fight fire with fire. Some will die but in the end all will profit from what I do. They'll thank me and erect great statues in my honour. Do you understand what I'm saying Presela?" said Kamahl.

"Yes I do," she said immediately.

"That's good, now run along and try hard to get me something I can use; use for the sake of humanity," said Kamahl.

Did he really believe what he just said or was he trying to convince her? Presela thought it was a little of both. Kamahl would in his magical way persuade someone not committed one way or another or someone wishing a cause to live for. Presela wanted nothing to do with him or his ways. She was a Seer and if anyone in this world knew what he truly was and represented then it was she. He was wasting his time with her.

# THE GIFTED OF SISCERLY VIII
*Alligators and Snakes*

THE WEATHER WARMED CONSIDERABLY as they descended the mountains. Summer finally took the bite out of the winter cold. Katie took off her pants teasing Shaun while doing so, pulling her robe higher than was necessary. She looked happy to be wearing her blue robe and snake belt, thighs exposed as she straddled her mount, teasing Shaun as she went. She was a witch and Shaun would be wise to bear that in mind. Witches did what witches did; some of it made no sense to Jensen at all.

The trip out of the pass was more gradual than the one in. Trees were more abundant and taller soon changing from softwood to hardwood. Slowly the woods grew dense and high, huge willows crowded the road. Water laid at the sides of the trail; not lakes or ponds only large bogs everywhere. Black pools of stagnant water were in abundance and actually moved or something in them did. The air was thick, humid, and harder to breathe. Branches arched over the path allowing little light to shine through. Katie stopped before a long bough not ducking under it, only looking up. In the dim light Jensen saw a long thick snake twisted around the branch, its tongue flickering. It slithered slowly to the other side away from Katie not taking its eyes off her. It was twice as long as she was tall and almost as big around as her waist. The sight made Jensen squirm but seemed to have little effect on Katie.

They came to a clearing and Katie dismounted stretching and arching her back after the long ride.

"Let's eat, I'm hungry," said Katie.

"I hope there aren't many snakes like that around," said Jensen pointing back to the tree.

"Sorry, the swamp is thick with them. This is where I was bitten by junior," said Katie pointing at her snake belt.

"How long before we get out of this?" asked Jensen.

"We don't. This is Cameria," said Katie.

"The whole country is like this?" said Jensen, her nose crinkled.

"There's clearings here and there but yah, that's the way it is," said Katie.

"The wizard can have it then," said Jensen.

As she was pronouncing those words Jensen saw a log on feet move toward the water hole where she had only a moment ago filled her canteen. She walked closer and saw its jaws open, enough teeth to cut her in two. Jensen jumped back and drew her dagger, too shocked to speak.

"That's an alligator. There's lots of those too," said Katie.

"Let's find Corel and get out of here. The place gives me the creeps," said Jensen.

"We won't make Scully Point till tomorrow. We'll have to find a place to camp later on," said Katie.

"In this place? Not me," said Jensen.

Jensen rode Biscuit along the winding trail looking for gators as Katie called them, hand on her dagger at every sound. She didn't know whether to look up in the trees for snakes or down to the ground for other evils in abundance here.

"Don't touch the spiders with the red cross on their bellies. They're deadly," shouted Katie as she swatted something on her shoulder.

Oh great thought Jensen as she looked around her then up and down. She couldn't have enough eyes in her head in a place like this.

The landscape changed as hills came into view and a large meadow they were crossing led to a dense forest beyond. The sun was at the apex of its climb and starting its descent as they rode along the narrowing trail into the bush. This section of the woods was hilly and slightly drier with tall maple and oak on either side of the path. One tree grew into the other above creating a canopy that shut out the pale blue sky and turned this world into a huge shadow. A few beams of light shone through the gaps between the leaves, barely enough to find their way. They were in a valley and hills on either side blocked light hampering them even more. It grew chilly the further into the woods they went.

Nothing grew beneath the dense overgrowth above: no bushes or shrubs, and only a few blades of grass here and there. The growl of something enraged sounded to their left and the last anguished scream of something else was cut off a second later. A frightened deer bounded across the trail before them and disappeared into the woods.

A branch snapped behind them and not long after that another one. Their horses started to run but were held in check until a loud growl confirmed they were being stalked. The reins were let slack and their mounts fled. They weaved and ducked as they galloped along the narrow trail afraid to look back. Katie pulled up her horse and the others did too as a steep ridge appeared before them.

"We'll have to dismount and walk the horses up," said Katie.

Before they could get a step farther a large bear appeared not far behind. He rose to his hind legs and threatened swinging his paws then moved their way with a growl. The horses were gone a second later. Katie took off her snake belt and it turned into a spear which she thrust at the bear as he swung his great paw. Shaun pulled out his sword and stood at Katie's side stabbing toward their enemy. Jensen drew her dagger stared at its inadequate length and wondered why she pulled it out in the first place. She sheathed it then stepped toward the bear behind Katie and Shaun and looked into its eyes.

"Go away, shoo, don't bother us," yelled Jensen. It was the only help she was able to afford.

The bear looked at her dropped to all fours and walked away.

"He was a male bear, that's why he listened," said Jensen.

"Yah right. I think he realized it was not going to be an easy meal to get," said Shaun.

"The horses ran up the ridge, let's find them," said Katie.

After a long walk they found their horses in another small meadow munching grass. They rested and all sat close together leaning against trees.

It was the strangest land Jensen had ever seen. Its changing landscape and variety of trees, its dense forests and inky pools were new to the inhabitant from Cambells Cross. Katie seemed to take its violent and dangerous wildlife with ease, almost as though it was boring to her. She was the anchor that held Jensen and Shaun in place. Jensen knew that had it not been for Katie's strength she would be unable to go on. She would have lost her sanity and run panic stricken for home; wherever that was today. And that's why she was here. She had no home and wanted the old one back.

"Are we out of the woods now Katie?" asked Jensen.

"No, believe it or not it gets even denser from here."

That's all Jensen needed to hear but then she'd asked and Katie never softened the truth.

"This is the most disgusting land I've ever seen," said Jensen with a scowl.

"How many have you seen?" asked Katie.

"Well, that's not the point, name one worse," said Jensen.

"The jungles of Anguitar where cats as big as horses roam and the deserts of Sara Gettey where never any water flows," said Katie.

"I've never even heard of those places much less been there before," said Jensen.

"My point. You only know Cambells Cross," said Katie.

"All right, but you can't make me like it here by telling me there's someplace worse," said Jensen.

"It's not all bad. Legend has it that this is the land of the fairies. If you're lost in these woods they'll help you find the way," said Katie.

"What do they look like?" asked Jensen.

"Legend says they're slight, thin, and smaller than us. They can glow in the darkness of the forest, lighting the way. They are creatures of magic and good will to those with pure hearts," said Katie.

"Have you seen them?" asked Jensen.

"Yes, when I was bitten by junior here, the swamp adder. They were the ones who saved me. I know when I'm here they're watching over me. If I'm in trouble they'll come," said Katie.

"So that's why you're so at ease," said Jensen.

"There's always someone to help Jensen. If you're in need then someone will come if you believe," said Katie.

"Did you talk to the fairies?" asked Jensen.

"Yes I did. The queen's name was Estelle. She was dainty with hair of shimmering gold," said Katie.

Shaun leaned forward and said, "I've heard tales where they lure men into the woods and use them as mates. Years later after they're done with them and find someone else they release them. They're mad when they return from the forests."

"Is that your dream Shaun? To be captured and used as a slave mate?" asked Jensen with a giggle.

"I'm serious, it's true," said Shaun.

"All I'm saying is that no matter how gloomy your world there's always some good in it as long as you believe. If you believe the world to be all evil then that's what you find," said Katie.

"You're not a man. You don't have to worry about being dragged into the bush and being used as a slave," said Shaun.

Jensen laughed out loud and could see Katie holding back from doing the same.

Jensen looked at Katie and wondered if her stories about the fairies were true. Jensen knew if she asked she would still be in the dark as Katie never answered a question without leaving a person guessing the truth.

"Katie were you just kidding or did you really see fairies," asked Jensen.

"Jensen, would I lie to you?" said Katie.

Jensen knew she would do that, answer a question with another. But that's what witches did; you could never tell what they were thinking, whether what they said was true or not.

They mounted refreshed and rested riding toward the dark wood beyond.

The land levelled and was flat as before with inky pools of water everywhere. They reached a forest almost black in colour with eyes that watched them from behind every tree. The tree trunks were dark with long branches that grew into each other forming a canopy denser than the last one they had previously left. These trees were higher than any before and were of a kind Jensen had not seen. The leaves were a gloomy green and shut off nearly all light leaving dimly lit tunnels running between the trunks. The passageways were as high as five men and three times as wide unobstructed by other growth as little sunlight broke through. The ground was moist but not muddy; no sound from the horses hooves as they went. Strange calls, shrieks and the hooting of owls or weird birds came from within.

Out of the darkness a black cloud moved their way, Jensen ducked as it flew overhead. They were bats as large as foxes with the wing span of eagles. The bats circled then dove toward them again as though inspecting their quarry. The horses bolted and turned, then stopped, only snorting not knowing which way to run. Jensen pulled the light crystal from her pocket and removed it from its pouch. She held the crystal high and it flashed bright as the noonday sun for a second. The flying foxes screamed in pain and left as quickly as they arrived.

"It's another gateway to the underworld. They say there are thirteen in all. It's darker in here than the last time I passed. The world of the dead is expanding," said Katie.

Jensen heard the cry of a baby and stopped. She dismounted and walked toward a dark grove of trees, the light fading to darkness beyond.

"I heard it too Jensen, ignore it, come back here," cried Katie.

"I can't, it's a baby, just behind this tree," said Jensen.

Jensen saw Katie dismount and come her way but decided to peek behind the tree.

"No Jensen."

It was the last sound she heard as she stepped behind the tree and walked out of this world into another.

# THE GIFTED OF SISCERLY IX
*The world of the dead*

JENSEN LOOKED FOR THE baby but found none; only a grey world made entirely of mist. Jensen saw no trees or rocks, nothing but fog. Haunting screams of torment sounded all around her even from the direction she came. Jensen turned to go back as she was only two steps within. She walked ten but found no exit so stopped not knowing which way to go. The grey figure of a man appeared before her; he was not whole and certainly not one of the living. She drew her dagger as he moved close but the blade did not shine blue. She pushed here hands into his boney chest and looked into the hollow spaces where his eyes had once been. She commanded that he stop but proceeded backing her as he grasped her arms.

Jensen broke free of his grip knowing for certain that the magic of her world had no affect in the realm of the dead. In an effort to escape she ran into the arms of another and saw more coming to from the depth of the mist.

All seemed lost to Jensen, her mind was a blank. She felt like a rabbit in the mouth of a wolf. She gasped for air and was lost in doom. Then Katie knocked down the grey man holding her and pulled Jensen out of harm's way. Katie had a rope tied to her waist which they followed and were soon out of the mist. Shaun appeared before her holding the rope's other end. They watched while he tugged it as though it had snagged. Shaun pulled hard and a grey figure emerged through the mist holding the rope not willing to release his grip. Jensen clutched the grey shape by the throat. Upon her touch it crumbled to dust; the ashes disappearing as well.

"Once in that dark realm there is no way out unless you keep contact with the other side," said Katie.

She pulled at the rope and it shrunk into a snake belt that she tied around her waist.

"I found that magic doesn't work there either," said Jensen.

"Only the Keepers black kind," said Katie.

They followed Katie ignoring all sounds trying to lure them into the mist. They heard the cry of loved ones and the calls of help from tortured children. Jensen heard the screams of her mother pleading for release. All had tears in their eyes as they left the sounds behind and rode into the sunlight away from the Keeper and his world. The flying foxes followed but kept their distance now refusing to pursue into sunlight. They flew in the shadows of the trees from one to another, their eyes glued on all three.

The three found a clearing on a hill, one of the few slopes Jensen had seen in this land. The horses were hobbled and greedily ate the lush grass. Jensen looked for firewood poking every log she saw with a stick before she dared go near it. Shaun cut up the longer branches with his sword. The young man had run from every fight so far but did stand up to the bear. He had no way out. There was nothing else he could do. Katie defended him none the less. She was sitting close to him teasing him again. Jensen couldn't understand the strange attachment she had to the young man.

Jensen grabbed the canteens and went to a nearby water hole. She sunk the first one into the water. Katie walked her way grabbing her by the shoulder and yanked her from the pond. Just as she did there was a snap and the canteen was gone held between two huge jaws.

"Alligators hide at the water's edge. The two eyeballs floating near shore are a dead giveaway," said Katie.

Jensen trembled unable to speak or move; only stared at the monster that almost took off her arm. The wizard couldn't want a land such as this. If he did who would be stupid enough to fight for it.

"I'll take first watch. A gator will walk right into a camp so watch your butt," said Katie.

"That's alright Katie I'll stand watch all night. I won't sleep a wink anyway," said Jensen.

"Are you sure girl?"

"Yah, thanks to gators, snakes, and spiders I may never sleep again," said Jensen.

Jensen watched Katie and Shaun as they slept, seemingly without care. It was a long night feeding the fire and looking round and round until she was almost too dizzy to see. Jensen's heart sank and she swallowed hard as the flying foxes passed close overhead. They must have followed them here. Were they the eyes of the Wizard?

Jensen saw a strange light as though figures were moving her way. Were they images of ghosts, people lost in this place of snakes and bogs? Were they servants of the Gods coming to take her to the land beyond? Was this the end of her life, a life not yet fulfilled? She would not leave. She'd fight even the Gods until her family was free.

"Who are you and what do you want," said Jensen.

"It's only me Estelle and my people. We've blinded the bats to your presence so worry no more. They can no longer report what they see. We know you're here on a noble cause so pass through this land without fear. Good bye for now and if you ever have need of us again please know we are here."

The figures rushed back and forth then were lost in the dark. Jensen could not believe her eyes or her ears. Did she fall asleep and dream it? Was she tired and hallucinating? She would never know for sure if it was real. Then she remembered what her mother used to say, "Jensen believe in your heart. The truth is there warm and sound, believe in your heart."

"Good bye Estelle and thank you," said Jensen.

Morning came, not soon enough for her, a thousand emotions and thoughts clouded her mind. Time would sort out these things, yes, it would take time. She tossed in the last of firewood then woke Katie and Shaun checking under their blankets for snakes and spiders. She saddled the three horses and was ready to go before the other two finished eating.

Katie walked her way a warm smile on her face, "You alright girl?"

"Yah, I'll be alright, don't worry."

They made Scully Point that afternoon as Katie had said. Jensen looked upon the houses large and solid made only of stone. The roofs were covered with clay tiles and the doors were solid oak. It was the prettiest village she'd ever seen.

They left their horses at the stable and went to the local

inn, Katie in the lead. She ordered ale and downed the glass in one gulp as everyone looked on.

"Another one and one for my friends."

Jensen took a drink from the large glass and ran out to the street spitting it on the road in front of three men walking in. It tasted like lamp oil to her. She walked in and pushed the glass aside.

"Water please."

"Trust me, you get used to it," said Katie.

"We're looking for a man named Corel," said Jensen to the barkeeper.

"You won't find him here."

"Why?"

"Because he left two days ago."

# THE GIFTED OF SISCERLY X
## *The dead man*

PRESELA HAD SEEN A man enter Kamahl's study more than once and wondered what he had to do with the wizard. The reason she wanted to know was because of the look of him. He was tall and thin with skin the colour of death and smelled of it.

Presela was sure he was dead.

She could not read his mind, he was a blank. He was as empty as the vase on the table beside her. Presela felt another force within him, driving and inhabiting his mind but could not find where that voice came from. She couldn't read Kamahl either but that was for another reason; he blocked her and trying to read his mind hurt. He would send pain her way if she even tried. He was a wizard after all.

Presela would send a spy, Cromby, and find out who he was and what he meant to Kamahl. If the wizard saw the cat he would think it had run off and pay him no mind. She would try to manoeuvre him in such a way that he would not be seen. Besides which the cat was a natural hunter and would soon be wary of the fact that he was stalking someone and should hide.

With Cromby gone she would be blind so needed to hide in a hall closet. If someone watched her she would never know. She sent Cromby on his way concentrating on what he saw and keeping him hidden as much as possible. He had a deep dislike for the wizard and wanted to stay out of his sight. Cromby hid out of view behind a cabinet. Presela listened to the conversation between Kamahl and the dead man.

"So it's all set then," she heard the wizard say.

"You'll have help from the Great One when you show him you have something to offer," said the dead man.

"I promise."

"You promise. He pays no attention to promises. Humans promise him all manner of things and then back out. He wants something from you and that is souls. If you can deliver then he'll help but don't promise, just do it," said the dead man.

"I need these people for work and for war. When I've won he can have all the damn souls he wants but I have to win first," said Kamahl.

"Your problems are of no concern to him. I told you that he wants payment first and then he'll help," said the dead man.

"All right I'll give him all I can."

"Remember that in order for the souls to become his they have to relinquish their own Gods first," said the dead man.

"Yes I know. In my dungeons I can persuade any man to do anything I want in return for a quick death."

"Then I'll go and leave it to you."

"Yes, and I'll give him two thousand souls this week, I promise," said Kamahl.

"Don't promise, just do," said the dead man.

When the man stood Presela called Cromby back. Cromby came to her quickly without complaint. He hated the wizard from the start. She should have listened to his instincts and left after the first day, but then he would not have let her go. His request for her to visit was no request, she knew that now. He wanted her and was going to have her. Presela was a prisoner before she even arrived after he decided he wanted her gift. Were there others like her? Maybe everyone disliked the man, but to seek out others could mean torture or death.

So the dead man really was a dead man and Kamahl was making a pact with the Dark One, Lord of the Underworld. In trade for souls he would get help with his wars. What kind of help though? Would he get dead men to fight in his war? Those thoughts were frightening as the dead outnumber the living. Already dead they could not be killed. She had information but what would she do with it? She would have to try to send it to someone, but whom? Amie was the strongest in Tyhton. If she could get through to anyone it would be her.

# THE GIFTED OF SISCERLY XI
## *The Highwaymen*

STILL TWO DAYS BEHIND Corel Jensen needed sleep so they would have to spend the night in Scully Point. The horses also needed rest and oats as they had none since the beginning of their journey.

"Do you know where he went," asked Jensen.

"Yup, the capital Kingstown. That's what he told me anyway," said the barkeep.

"How far is that Katie?" asked Jensen.

"Two days."

"Oh no, not another night out there," said Jensen.

"Yah, if you want to go."

"Do you have three rooms?" asked Jensen.

"Yup."

"What about something to eat?" asked Katie.

"Got that too."

They ate and Jensen went to her room jumped into bed and slept until Katie shook her next morning.

"Let's go if you ever want to catch him," said Katie.

"I've got to buy something, I'll be back in a minute," said Jensen to the others.

Jensen walked to the general store at the end of the street. Every place had one and the variety of goods they sold depended on the number of inhabitants it served. This one had a fine selection of clothes and boots, saddles and bridles, with a feed store attached. She found meat, bread, and cheese but not what she was looking for. Oh, finally there it was the weapon section. She looked at swords and daggers then finally found what she needed. It was a solid steel club about the length of her forearm with a round spiked metal head. It was a little heavy but she could get used to it. It was the perfect club to keep alligators in line. She would lose her hand trying to stab one with her dagger, magic or not. She also picked out some bread, meat, and cheese for the journey.

"I'll take this club and the food," said Jensen to the attendant.

"That's a mace."

"Yes of course, that's what I mean, mace."

"One gold mark."

Jensen paid and went to the stable where Katie and Shaun waited, Biscuit was already saddled.

"It's a gator mace," said Jensen defensively before either could say a word.

"Who's going to swing it for you," said Shaun.

Jensen took the mace in both hands and swung it over her shoulder like an axe and pounded it firmly into the ground inches from Shaun's foot. Shaun jumped as it drove home beside him.

"I used to split wood at home, it was one of my daily chores," said Jensen.

Jensen tied the mace to her saddle and mounted. They left for Kingstown only two days and one night away. The way out was the same as the way in; willow trees and all manner of huge vegetation that grows near swamps along the trail, few bushes in sight. Gators and snakes roamed freely at the side of the road and at times across or along it, no fear in their eyes only rage. This was their world and not hers. She didn't want to fight them for it, only pass in one piece.

Jensen wondered why Katie looked so at home in this place and knew there must be more of a story to that than she was telling. Shaun lived off Katie's strength so if she was calm then so was he. He always rode close to her and knew that if trouble came she would come to his aid. He would never be a knight unless Katie made him one.

They found a clearing and stopped for food Jensen had bought at the store; salted meat but different varieties than they were used to.

"This is good and spicy, what is it?" asked Jensen.

"Snake," said Katie.

Jensen didn't know whether to believe her or not but stopped eating nonetheless. She heard the sound of horses coming their way then watched as four men rode into view.

"Highwaymen. There's too many for us. We'll have to see if we can buy our way out," said Katie.

They all stopped then one of the men dismounted and walked toward them, the others slowly surrounding them.

"You wouldn't happen to have a little extra food would you?" asked one that looked to be the leader.

"Sure, here's all we have left," said Katie and graciously handed him the sack.

"You wouldn't also have a little gold or silver would you?" asked the highwayman.

"We have a gold coin for you," said Katie.

"Only one?"

"Yah, only one."

"You wouldn't be holding out on me now would you?" asked the highwayman. He came closer to Katie and the rest of the men followed.

"Give him a coin Jensen and be nice put it right in his hand don't be rude and throw it," said Katie with the wink of an eye.

Jensen got the message and for some reason the deal was off; they wouldn't buy their way out of this. She pulled a coin from her pocket and walked over to the man placing her hand over his. She reached up with her other hand and toughed his chest over his heart. The surge of her gift ran through her hand and into him.

"Take your men and go away, now."

The man looked like he had eyes made of stone and didn't even blink. He dropped the coin and told his men to mount up. They moved his way confused and argued. Jensen went to Biscuit and untied the mace then watched as Katie undid her belt. She was holding it in one hand letting the other end drag on the ground. The leader fought with his men and was quickly killed, the others looking down at his body in confusion.

The confusion didn't last long enough to suit Jensen. They were walking her way. She came out from behind Biscuit mace in hand. Katie shook the belt, turning it into a gold sword. The move startled the highwaymen but didn't stop them. Jensen ran at the first to come her way. She swung the mace at his head but the man stepped aside, the mace pounding into the dirt. He swung his sword causing Jensen to duck as the sword whistled over her head. Through the corner of her eye she saw Katie's sword smash into her assailant's chest. She owed the witch another one. Jensen rose to her feet and watched as Shaun engaged the last one. A highwayman was trying to cut down Katie backing her toward the woods. Katie had no problem with only one attacker and soon finished him. The witch swung with the fury of a man and backed him to his death. Shaun was only holding his own. The highwayman seeing that he was the last ran for his horse and rode away. Jensen hugged Katie then Shaun; he'd pulled his sword and fought.

The rest of the day went without incidence. Jensen was unable to sleep so stood guard all night long. By the end of the second day they were in Kingstown. Only able to find two rooms, Shaun took one leaving the two women to share a bed. Jensen ate and immediately went to her room, jumped into bed and fell asleep.

Jensen felt her shoulder being tugged and woke to see Katie vigorously shaking her.

"What's wrong," asked Jensen.

"Corel has been taken to Kyber Keep and jailed."

"Where? Why?"

"Kyber Keep, a prison. They say he got drunk and killed somebody. From what I heard it was self defence," said Katie.

"Can we get him out?"

"No one has ever left the Keep alive."

"What do we do?"

"We'll take a look at daybreak. Get some sleep," said Katie.

The next morning Jensen was too upset to eat, her knight

was in prison. The man she needed to save Cambells Cross was behind bars. They retrieved their horses from the stable and set out for Kyber Keep. Not far from town they found the infamous tower. It stood alone on a small patch of desert probably created by magic as the rest of the land lay within a swamp. No one could even get close except at night.

"The walls are as thick as a man is high," said Katie.

"Can you get in using magic?" asked Jensen.

"Maybe. The walls are also protected by magic, what kind I don't know. It probably won't have any affect on you though," said Katie.

"We'll come back tonight."

Jensen fumbled with a rope but knew it would be of little use against magic. If the way was blocked by a wizard's or a sorceress's spell man made tools would be useless. An impenetrable wall would surround the keep and only one of great power would get through. Jensen and Katie were not in their league, not even close.

# THE GIFTED OF SISCERLY XII
## *Kyber Keep*

THE DAY WORE ON slowly and was filled with questions from Katie about Cambells Cross. Jensen knew she was only trying to keep her mind busy but small talk on a day such as this made her irritable. They were about to enter a domain guarded by men of evil and protected by the magic of a wizard.

Night finally came and they approached the Keep. No men guarded the entrance and none walked the ramparts. Shaun gladly stayed with the horses as he had no immunity whatsoever to the magic that awaited them. Both Jensen and Katie would have a chance.

Jensen crept through the dark night and Katie followed. At the front gate Jensen approached the door but Katie was unable to pass. It was as though she had run into a wall.

"I'm going in alone. I'll come back if I run into danger," said Jensen.

"Take care."

Jensen tested the latch, feeling her power flow slowly through it. The door creaked open. There were no metal bars holding it shut, only magic that her gift had the power to overcome. She walked to the tower and tested the entrance, her hands running over and around the thick wood. It also sprung open for her. She gasped as a man grabbed her hand on entering. Jensen did not fight him only drew herself into him and touched his chest. Her power flowed and his eyes went blank.

"Take me to Corel Blue, the knight brought here three days ago."

Jensen followed close as he led her through corridors, down aisles, and through doors to and area filled with cells. The imprisoned men watched with wide eyes. They said nothing.

"He's in there," said the guard.

Jensen looked through a small window in the entrance leading to a corridor. Another guard stood at a cell near the end of the hall. Jensen knew she would be spotted and he would alert others. She was so close and yet it seemed an insurmountable problem to her. No way to get Corel out she would have to return or be captured and tortured or worse. It all seemed like a mean trick the God's had played on her.

"Jensen use your will."

Jensen heard the sounds that were like a whisper, the sound of Kenji's voice directly in her right ear.

"Look into his eyes, his soul and will him to bring Corel to you. Your gift is strong."

"I thought you never interfered in the struggles of men," whispered Jensen.

"Shhh. I only help a friend," Kenji whispered.

Jensen looked to the guard twenty paces away; looked into his eyes and searched for his soul. She commanded him to bring Corel to her side. Jensen stared until she saw only his eyes and whispered her commands over and over. Then she felt her power flow from her eyes to his. His head went back as he reeled and fought to stand.

The guard shook his head from side to side then a moment later took out a key and opened the door behind him. He retrieved a big man from the cell and brought him to her.

"Are you Corel," Jensen asked.

"Yes."

She looked into his green eyes and handsome face and was immediately attracted to him. Only the urgency of the moment broke her stare.

"Come with me," she said and he followed.

Jensen ordered the guards to stay and quickly walked down the corridors from whence she came followed closely by the knight. Jensen stepped into the courtyard and was spotted by four guards on patrol. They ran her way drawing swords. Staring into the lead soldier's eyes she commanded him to stop the others. He turned and arms out held back his comrades only one racing by. That one was almost upon her sword in hand. Jensen stared at him and commanded that he stop. There was not enough time, it was too late. Corel's fist sent the man to the ground. Jensen walked out the front gate Corel her knight close behind.

Katie jumped into Corel's arms kissing him on the mouth, "Hello big guy."

"Let's get out of here," said Jensen.

"Corel can ride with me," said Katie.

Jensen rode ahead then looked back to make sure the others followed. Katie sat behind Corel her arms rapped around the knight's waist, her head leaning on his left shoulder. By the look of the man Jensen knew her friend would not tease him.

The knight looked like someone who took what he wanted. That handsome face, those green eyes, and long dark hair had melted the hearts of many a maiden.

They rode back to the inn at Kingstown; Corel stayed hidden in the shadows and darkness of doorways. Jensen went to the stable where she bought another horse. Katie retrieved their clothes and valuables from their room. They rode from town to find a place where an escape plan could be made. The guards at the keep would not let this matter lie as their reputation was at stake. They would follow for certain and would not easily be shied away. They found a clearing far from town and started a fire.

"Where to?" asked Jensen.

"The sea. There is only one road in and out of town so it will be well covered," said Corel.

"They'll be watching the ships as well," said Katie.

"Not the ones they don't know about. Not the smugglers," said Corel.

"Do you know smugglers?" asked Jensen.

"Of course. It's my business to know things like that," said Corel.

The more Jensen learned about him the more she liked the man, "Have you finished your business here?"

"Yes, I asked for and alliance and they turned me down. They don't think Kamahl will come," said Corel.

"They may be right. I've seen enough of their country to know that I wouldn't want it," said Jensen.

"Kamahl will take whatever is in front of him and this place will be next if Tyhton falls," said Corel.

Jensen smiled as she followed Corel on her way to find a shipload of smugglers. What would the folks at home think of her now? She had a lot of faith in that man and felt the safety of her family was possible with his help as well.

Presela could see Amie getting ready for bed although she was a thirty miles west. As soon as she relaxed would be a good time to attempt contact with her. Presela would have to do it before Amie fell asleep as anything after that the sorceress would think was a dream. Presela whispered Amie's name over and over.

"Amie, can you hear me?"

In her mind she saw Amie rise and sit on the side of her bed with her brow tight and straining to hear.

"Amie, can you hear me, nod if you can."

Presela watched Amie still sitting on the side of the bed looking around the room.

"Amie, I'm not in the room but I can see you. I'm Presela a Seer. If you can hear me say yes."

"Yes."

Presela hugged Cromby and gave the cat a kiss making him to purr.

"All right Amie, listen, I'm being held by Kamahl. My mother and I are prisoners. He's making me give information on Jensen and your people. I don't want to do it. I'm going to try to escape, get myself and my mother out and come to Tyhton."

"No, not without help. We have people inside. I'll send one to you so wait. Do you hear?"

"Yes, I hear."

"Good bye for now and wait for help," said Amie.

Presela could hardly believe what she had done but was totally drained and would have to sleep.

Amie dressed and shot out of her bedroom leaving the palace in haste. She had to find Mira. The witch would be in a tavern on the other side of town half drunk by now. Hopefully the old girl could still stand and be able to walk. She was a crusty old witch but of great value to Tyhton being accepted by all including Kamahl. Amie found her with three of her friends all about fifty years old. Amie was the same age as them, all a member of the over fifty group on the castle grounds. They offered Amie a drink but she told Mira there was urgent business to be had. Amie dragged the old girl back to the palace where they would talk.

"What's this all about Amie, the night's just begun?" asked Mira.

"I need your help. I need you to get two people out of Kamahl's palace. A Seer Presela and her mother and bring them here."

"Is that all, get Presela. He won't let her go easily you know."

"Do you know her?" asked Amie.

"Yes, but she's one of his top advisors. Do you think it a trick?"

"No. if I thought that at all I'd never ask you to get her out."

"How do you know?"

"Because she contacted me and told me things, things she didn't have to."

"All right, I'll try but in the morning old friend."

"Good night dear."

Amie knew the old witch was going back to the tavern to be with her friends. Once a favour had been promised by her old friend she would be on her way in the morning to carry it out. Mira was a lush but one with a good heart. Nikita was excited beyond words when she heard the news. With the help of a Seer they would have a better chance of stopping Kamahl. They hoped Mira could get her out.

# THE GIFTED OF SISCERLY XIII
*The Smugglers*

THEY RODE TOWARD THE coast, Corel in the lead. Patrols had to be avoided which meant riding into the dangerous swamp at times. Jensen felt weak and drained of energy. Taking control of the soldier's minds at a distance was not without cost. Had there been more men her dagger would have been the weapon of necessity.

Corel certainly knew his way around thought Jensen. He was such a likable soul she wondered how the man could possibly be a dangerous knight. There must be another side to the man; one Jensen had never seen.

The smell of the sea was in the air, seagulls soaring above. Jensen could not believe her eyes as they approached a huge wooden vessel. It was larger than the meeting hall at Cambells Cross. She used to sit in that hall listening to the speeches of village elders and thought there were few places in the world that big. Fully packed it could hold almost a hundred people. Now she was looking at a ship grander than that.

Both ends of the vessel were higher than the middle with

long masts stretching into the sky supporting sails, rigging, and flags. Leading to the centre of the ship was a long ramp where sailors were unloading goods. They were finally spotted; the men stood defensively defying them to come closer. Corel held up his hand to signal a halt and dismounted walking their way unarmed. A large man wearing baggy clothes came his way arms wide then hugged Corel. Both danced in circles slapping each other's back then shook hands. Jensen smiled proud to have a smuggler as a friend. Who else did he know? He was without doubt the most exciting man she had ever met.

Corel called the others as his arm wrapped around the shoulders of the smuggler.

"Meet my friend Sly Stone captain of this vessel. We call him Sly as he's run every King's blockade under the sun," said Corel.

"And I've never been boarded by any of the King's men," said Sly.

"If he had they'd never leave the ship alive," said one of his men.

All the sailors broke into a roar of laughter. Jensen wondered why?

Jensen led Biscuit up the ramp into a place Corel called the hold. There were enough stalls for ten horses. She led and securely tied Biscuit in one. Sailors fastened extra ropes around the horse's rump to further secure the little mare. Jensen returned to the upper deck and joined Katie at the end of the ship.

"Is this the front end or the back?" asked Jensen.

"The pointy end is the front, so this is it. It's called the bow and the back is the stern," answered Katie.

"Where are we going?"

"Sharks Way."

"Your home."

"I don't have a home."

"Where were you born?"

"I don't know. Maybe I wasn't."

"You had to be born. Everyone's born," said Jensen thinking Katie's voice had an empty ring to it like someone who wanted to be heard.

"My first memories go back about fifteen years. I guess I was about twenty then, full grown."

"Where did your magic come from?"

"It was just there from the first day that I can remember."

"I can control men. What kind is yours?"

"Hah, you've probably noticed I can reshape things. That's all."

"That's enough. Can you reshape people?"

"No, too complex a package. I wouldn't know where to start."

Jensen waited for more but nothing else came. She would not push Katie. She would say more when ready.

"What are they doing?"

"We're getting underway."

The ramp was pulled aboard and the sails rose. Jensen was more than a little happy to avoid the return trip through the swamp. The alligators and snakes could find someone else to frighten; she'd had enough of them for a lifetime. Jensen looked high as more sails were raised on the six masts. A flag with skull and crossbones upon it was raised to the very top of the highest one.

Jensen stood beside Katie the wind blowing her hair straight back. The cool sea air was fresh on her face whisking the swamp smells from her body.

Jensen laughed at men climbing to the top of the masts then swinging from one to another securing the riggings. She looked to the sea and watched large fish jump from the water. Salty sprays wetted her face and clothes as the ship cut through the sea ever faster. The seagulls were leaving which meant shore was far behind.

Jensen watched Shaun on the deck below follow Corel and the captain wherever they went. He was trying so hard to fit in but somehow looked out of place in their company. It was the first time she had seen Corel wearing a sword. It made him look dangerous not only handsome. His tall muscular frame stood out from the others; the sword and dagger added even more excitement to his look.

"What do you know of Corel, Katie?" asked Jensen.

"He's every woman's dream, don't get hung up on him. He's there one minute and gone the next."

"It sounds like you love him."

"Oh, I think every woman loves him and he in turn loves all women."

"I like him a lot. Does he have magic?"

"Yah, The kind that draws women to him, nothing more."

"You seem to like Shaun too."

"Shaun's like a lost puppy. He needs help. A little jolt to put him on track."

Jensen smiled as it was the first time Katie had loosened up and said what she thought about herself and everyone else.

Jensen's brow tightened as she looked to the horizon turning black.

"Look how dark the sky is over there."

Jensen gazed upon the black sky moving their way as though driven by magic. She was wearing the amulet so Kamahl could not know she was here. Maybe it was the way of things on the sea, sunshine one minute and rain the next. The shouts from sailors filled the air as they ran this way and that. They didn't seem lost in panic but were securing the ship for the upcoming storm. Most of the sails came down and were tied off. Work looked harder to do in the gale force winds that bore down on them. Jensen was pushed toward the hold frozen in shock of the overwhelming fury she was witness to. Jensen felt twice her weight fighting winds assaulting her. Feeling powerless against the forces exploding around her she followed Katie's lead.

Katie tied Jensen to a beam in the hold near Biscuit. The back of the ship rose high making her feel as though she was going downhill. Jensen held Katie tight as her friend had no time to tie herself. They levelled then the front went high as though climbing a steep hill. They rocked endlessly like sliding through a series of valleys.

Jensen strained to look at Biscuit behind her; the little mare screaming in terror. Seawater poured from the deck above knee high when the ship levelled which it seldom did. Jensen's hands and arms ached finding it hard to hold Katie's water soaked body but refused to let go.

The vessel jolted to Jensen's right, the left side coming high as more water than ever streamed into the hold. She felt the worst was yet to come as the ship was being knocked up and down, side to side. The roar of the sea, the screaming of winds, the groaning of straining lumber, and the shrieking of the horses rang through the air. Out of fear she clutched Katie ever tighter.

The sound of wood snapping and giving way filled the air; Jensen could think of no sound more fearful at this moment. A large explosion like thunder, then the ship came to an abrupt halt throwing her forward into the ropes. Jensen felt Katie slip from her grasp then all went black.

Jensen woke on a beach, the rain pouring down, Katie looking upon her.

"You look like crap Katie."

"I feel worse."

"What happened?"

"The ship ran aground on an island."

"Is everyone all right?"

"Four sailors dead or lost."

"Corel and Shaun?"

"Both bruised like us but all right."

"Biscuit?"

"The horses survived. They were well tied."

"Is the ship destroyed? Are we stuck here?"

"They can make repairs. I don't know how long it will take."

"We should have taken the swamp road back. There were only alligators, snakes, spiders, and highwaymen waiting there," said Jensen.

Jensen cursed the God's under her breath. She had found Corel and was bringing him back home to save her parents and now this. Depressed, Jensen walked up the ramp and into the hold. She petted Biscuit and fed the horses some hay then laid and fell asleep.

# THE GIFTED OF SISCERLY XIV
## *The Goddess*

ONE HAND SHIELDING HER eyes from the blinding sun Jensen walked down the ramp. Morning brought an end to the storm and peace to their world. She watched the men scurry about checking the ship for damage. The captain was overjoyed about something as he walked along the hull kissing it as he went. Half the masts were gone but she hoped they could sail with what was left.

"There's no major breaks in the hull," said Katie.

"I guess that's good."

"Oh yes, if there were we wouldn't leave here."

The sound of drums stirred something within Jensen. She looked to the forest far from the beach. A single mountain stretched above the dense woods. A procession of soldiers walked their way, two men wide in a straight line. Closer they came, Jensen straining to see more detail. They were carrying a large chair with someone sitting upon it. As they neared Jensen made out the face of a woman wearing a crown, holding an ornate stick with a blue diamond on top. She wore no smile; her face suggested no greeting would come forth.

"You will come with us," said the woman.

"We're only here to fix our ship then we'll be gone," said Corel.

She looked long and hard at Corel. Her appearance seemed to soften, a smile almost coming upon her, then as though angry at herself she looked away from him. Her face turned to stone.

"I said you will come with us," her tone leaving no doubt that it was no request.

Corel stepped forward and as he did she pointed the sceptre his way. A blue beam came from the diamond striking him in the chest. He fell to the ground. Jensen rushed to him, Katie was already there.

"He has a pulse. He's alive. Can you do anything with the soldiers?"

"There's too many and I'm still weak from the storm," said Jensen.

"Same here. There's too many so let's not show them what we have until the odds are on our side."

"All right we'll go with you," yelled Jensen at the woman.

"You speak for the men," she asked.

The captain looked around outnumbered four to one he only shrugged then nodded.

They followed their captors into the woods unbound. The trees were huge the likes of which Jensen had never seen. They were twice as tall as the tallest willow and three times as big around. The closer they came to the distant mountain the more it seemed an unnatural structure. It looked to be made by man not nature; it was too perfect a shape. Jensen looked behind, following her were twenty soldiers, another ten in the lead. The Queen held the sceptre close and looked ahead with no regard for what followed.

Soon they came to a wall, high and long, surrounding the mountain. The wall was the height of ten men and a huge wooden gate opened before them. They entered a city the man made peak standing in the centre. Around it stood shops and houses separated by gardens of flowers and bushes. Corn and wheat grew in fields left and right of the buildings, all within the confines of the long barricade. Stone walkways throughout circled the pyramid leading to steps running to its peak. People stared at the trespassers entering their realm.

They were taken to a building lavish in structure and not a jail cell as Jensen thought awaited them. They were led to pools of steaming water and encouraged to bathe by young women who attended their every need. The sailors smiled as though the Gods had finally answered their prayers and given them their just reward. Jensen looked to Katie who gave her a raised brow and shrug not knowing what to make of the whole affair.

At only sixteen Jensen knew that nothing was free. There was a hidden price to be paid for their comfort but she did not know what that was to be. Jensen looked at Katie again as her friend removed her robe and jumped into the pool naked. The sailors only watched their eyes glued to the sight afraid to touch a witch. Jensen modestly removed her clothing then dove in beside Katie drawing the attention of everyone there.

They were given a feast fit for a King and wine of their choice. Katie drank with the sailors and was still sitting when the last of them fell. Jensen sipped only one glass and was aware of her surroundings. She stood and walked toward the door but was blocked by two muscular guards. She looked into their eyes and asked them to step aside which they did. She strolled toward the tallest building where Corel had been taken and entered the front doorway. Guards again blocked her entry but upon gazing into her eyes denied her nothing. She slowly ambled through the corridors and finally found a room where Corel lay. He was still under a spell, his eyes glazed and not responsive to her voice. Jensen left the building and returned to her own wanting to consult Katie. Katie was dead to the world and Jensen thought she would be out for some time so lay down and slept as the others.

Morning light shattered the peace and silence as it pierced through the large windows surrounding the room. Men groaned, heads down avoiding the blinding light praying for the return of darkness. Jensen raised her brow as Katie hugged her knees, head upon them. The witch was twice her age yet had not learned to keep clear of alcohol; no one could win battling that poison. Guards ushered them to the pyramid and all were required to climb the thousand or so steps before them. Jensen walked with Katie at her side not knowing what to make of the ritual.

At the top Jensen looked around; she could see almost the whole island. There were no other mountains; it was an isle, only a sandy patch of land. Where did the rocks come from to build this pyramid? It had to be constructed of magic.

A sailor was taken to table made of stone and forced to lie upon it. A man dressed in white robes with a dagger walked toward him as the Queen looked on, stone faced as ever. Jensen thought him to be a priest of whatever God they worshipped. The Queen nodded and the dagger was raised over the sailor's chest. Jensen looked into the eyes of the priest and commanded him to stop. He did.

Jensen was more than a little pleased as the Queen went wild looking at everyone. She ordered the priest to proceed but he only stood staring, eyes blank. She ordered the man immediately beheaded; a guard doing as was directed. The priest slumped headless to the stone floor.

Another priest was directed to take his place and again Jensen told him to stand down. The Queen eyed everyone and stopped as she gazed at Jensen. Jensen looked around seeing that only she and Katie stood straight and unafraid; the heads of all others bent toward the ground.

The Queen pointed her sceptre at Jensen; a blue beam hit her in the chest. Jensen was knocked to the ground but rose again brushing the dust from her clothes. The Queen ordered the guards to take her out of the city and into the woods beyond. Katie stood by her side and walked with her. The Queen didn't protest; probably only wanted to be rid of a problem she couldn't comprehend.

Jensen and Katie were taken to the main entrance. The gates opened and twenty or so guards forced them out into the forest beyond. They were on their own in a world they knew nothing about. Both heard shrieks of pain and agony from the woods. No way back they reluctantly moved ahead wondering what the huge walls shielded the city from.

Mira's head hurt as the sun crept into her room. She was afraid to open her eyes but did knowing she had urgent business to attend. What was it she thought? Oh yes, Presela, that's right. Get the girl out. Mira found the basin and soaked her aching head and eyes. She stumbled making her way to the stables. Leaning on the walls and railings Mira found her way to the street. So far it was the worst morning of her life but then it was a thousand times she had had that thought before.

She managed a saddle on Chimneysweep, her pure black horse, and then struggled to mount.

"Let's go old boy. We got work to do."

Mira hated Kamahl but did work for him on occasion. He paid well and things she did hurt no one. Not long ago whether knowing or not a witch he had burned was a friend of hers. Mira had a score to settle with Kamahl. Not head to head as he was too strong but in the back; that's right she would get him when he wasn't looking.

Mira had taken the stallion, Chimneysweep, from a commander she had killed; the man who lit the fire when they burned, Julia, her friend. If she could hurt Kamahl in little ways like this, taking the Seer from him, then that would do Julia justice. That was one of Kamahl's problems; he didn't know what a friend was, never had one. He didn't know how far people would go for the ones they loved.

Mira was known by most soldiers on both sides so came and went at will. She made her way to Ravencroft, Kamahl's castle and town. Mira stabled her horse then got a room at the inn and had a drink or two, just to settle her nerves for the chore ahead. She met friends and had a long night. Mira had friends in every village and town.

Mira woke in the same state as the day before and the day before that. First she waited for her sight to return and then had to learn how to walk again. Mira managed her way to the palace and waited to see the wizard.

"You got any work for me Kamahl?"

"Yes, actually I have. Guarding some supply wagons headed for the troops on the border."

"Sure I'll take it. Same pay as before?"

"The same. Just see the paymaster when you're done. I'll give him the word."

"All right, see you later."

Mira left his study and went upstairs to see a friend who worked here as a maid. Mira had the run of the palace having several friends inside and out. No one thought twice about a drunken witch in any case. Mira walked by a room and in it saw Presela and her cat. She went in and shut the door behind her then looked around and saw no one else.

"Amie sent me to get you and your mother out."

"When?"

"Tonight I think. I just wanted you to know I was here. Get to your mother and tell her to get ready, take nothing, we go as is," said Mira.

"I can get out but mom can't. There's a guard at the door."

"The guard is nothing; it's getting out of the country that's tough. I'm going to hide you in a supply wagon I think. You don't drink do you?" said Mira.

"No, why?"

"Well if you do don't be drinking tonight," said Mira.

"All right."

Mira left to find the supply wagons and soon did. They would be loaded tonight and leave at dawn. She had it all worked out in her mind; the only problem was, how would she stay sober until way after dark. It would be a chore. In order to stay sober the first thing Mira had to do was to stay clear of her friends.

"Hey, Mira," she heard a friend say and knew it was Agnes a waitress at the inn.

"Oh Agnes no. I got to stay sober tonight so help me with that if you can," said Mira.

"And who's going to help me? You got a hot date or something?" asked Agnes.

"Let's go to your house, we'll stay away from the inn."

"How do you know I got nothing to drink at home?"

"Because if you did you wouldn't be out here," said Mira.

"You know me too well old girl."

They stayed in the house and drank nothing but tea, talked of old times and friends long gone. Agnes went to bed and so did Mira but made sure she did not fall asleep.

Well into the night Mira made her way to the castle. She knew the back way in, the doors the servants used, then in semi-darkness found Presela's room. The young woman was ready and waiting with her cat in the pocket of her travelling coat. Mira only wanted to make sure she was ready so told her to stay put. Mira walked down the aisle then put a soldier to sleep with a spell and opened the door. Presela had told her mother the plan and she was ready to go.

They made their way downstairs where Kamahl and a dozen of his soldiers stepped out of the study.

"Well well. Leaving are we?" said Kamahl.

"How did you know?" asked Presela.

"Your mother told me."

"Dear, you have a good position here, I couldn't let you just give it away," said her mother.

"You mean you've got a good position here, I'm the one who has to help him kill people not you," said Presela.

"Now now, and what of you Mira. Why would you defy me?" asked Kamahl.

"Remember Julia the witch you burned last winter, well, she was a friend of mine and this was the get even," said Mira.

"It looks more like another witch will burn tomorrow and maybe a Seer if she's no good to me. Take them both to the dungeons," ordered Kamahl.

Mira and Presela were taken to the dungeons and locked in a cell; their future looked bleak. No way out of this Mira thought.

# THE GIFTED OF SISCERLY XV
## *The Jungle*

JENSEN AND KATIE WALKED back toward the ship no idea what to do next. Jensen had little to say knowing the sailor would be long dead and others would be in peril. Strange sounds echoed around her, none of a familiar tone. Birds with strange curved beaks cawed like a crow. Others whistled as a man would; all larger than she was accustomed to. She looked to the sky for birds of prey, hawks, eagles and such but found none. Jensen searched the huge trees, three times larger than anything she'd ever seen, for familiar sights but found nothing of her world amongst those branches.

Jensen stopped in horror, both hands fisted in front of her mouth. A snake ten times her length wound its way along a bough above, its eyes meeting hers. Jensen stood motionless; a strange calmness washed over her body when flight should have been the only act. The snake moved closer, their eyes locked, terror filling her soul, yet unable to move. Jensen felt something pushing her backward and fell, staring at the sky above. It was Katie who'd shoved her out of harms way.

"Don't look one of those in the eyes," said Katie.

"What is it?" asked Jensen.

"It's an Anaconda. The largest snake you'll ever see," said Katie.

"Did you see them before?"

"Yes, another place, another time."

Jensen snuck along the trail looking left and right not advancing unless Katie did so, trying to hide behind her friend. They came to a swamp, the trail turning into a bridge made of stone. As they neared the crossing the largest alligator Jensen had ever seen moved through the tall rushes along the shore directly toward them. It was five times her length with the longest set of jaws holding what appeared to be a hundred teeth. On its short legs it scrambled their way making a growling sound as it went. Jensen ran for her life but fell over the knarred root of a tree spanning the trail. Katie was tugging Jensen's arm trying to pull her from danger. Jensen's world blurred; the jaws of death weren't far away. It was as though she was looking through tears then it all stopped. Everything froze as the transparent image of Kenji appeared before them.

"Fine mess you've gotten yourself into," said Kenji.

"We?" said Jensen.

"Yes you. Why did you let that silly woman run you out of her compound?"

"She had soldiers and that sceptre. There were too many for me to handle," said Jensen.

"Jensen the reason she ran you out was because you let her. Had you acted as an enchantress and not the victim you would have conquered," said Kenji.

"I don't understand. How can I take control of so many minds at once?" asked Jensen.

"You don't have to. Only act as though you control them. The leaders, the few that have the courage to come your way, take control of them. The others will follow their lead," said Kenji.

"What of the sceptre? I am not immune to it as Jensen," said Katie.

"Know that to be true and stay clear of its charge but what is it made of girl?" asked Kenji.

"Wood, I think with a diamond head," answered Katie.

"Think about that a minute," said Kenji.

"I've got it. I know what you mean," answered Katie.

"Good now go back and help your friends before more die for nothing as sacrifice to a God that never was," said Kenji.

"How do we get back in? The wall is ten men high and so is the gate," asked Katie.

"Katie, you always see things as a whole and not what makes it that. Do you need a gate ten men high and twenty wide to enter? I think not. You need only a space the size of a block of stone to enter," said Kenji.

"I see what you mean in that also. Thanks," said Katie.

"Together the two of you can conquer kingdoms greater than what you have encountered so go back and free your friends," said Kenji.

"Thanks for your help," said Jensen.

"I did not help, only counsel my only friends. I will not let you perish for lack of confidence," said Kenji.

"What about the gator?" asked Jensen.

"Katie, how do you light a fire?" asked Kenji.

"Got that one too, thanks," answered Katie.

"We women have to stick together in a world of men. Good bye for now and save your friends," said Kenji.

The transparent image of Kenji slowly disappeared before them and the world resumed as it had before.

Katie left Jensen and ran to the woods returning with a branch she caused to burst into flames. She shoved the burning ember toward the encroaching crocodile then gave it to Jensen. Katie soon returned with another and both drove the crocodile back into the reeds from whence it came.

"That was a crocodile. They're bigger than alligators," said Katie.

"Let's hope we don't meet any more," said Jensen.

Jensen followed Katie to the compound determined to free all those imprisoned. They soon came to the gate, the sun setting, little light remaining this day. Katie ignited some dry wood for light as they moved away from the gate to the stoned wall.

"What are you going to do?" asked Jensen.

"See this stone here. I am going to change this one little stone. I am going to make it longer and thinner," said Katie.

Jensen watched as Katie shifted the stone until it was ten times as long as her but only the width of her hand leaving a gap big enough for them to struggle through.

They both walked toward the collection of buildings housing their friends and entered. The guards were made friendly by Jensen's touch. The two ate ravenously making up for the meals missed all day.

In the morning the procession of Queen and guards made its way toward the steps leading to the top of the pyramid. Jensen walked toward the guards head high as though she commanded all. Captains walking her way were quickly tamed by her stare. Jensen's power flowed from her eyes to theirs. The others merely followed as Kenji said they would.

Jensen watched Katie close in on the Queen, both locked eyes on each other, murder in their hearts. The Queen raised her sceptre and Katie turned the wooden handle turned into a snake. A deadly Swamp Adder which bit the Queen. The self proclaimed Goddess died without a final battle ever being fought. No one but her had to die.

The soldiers would follow whomever Jensen chose as a leader. She picked a young maiden, one that she felt had compassion not greed or lust.

Corel was free of the Queen's spell as soon as her untimely death occurred. It was all as easy as Kenji had stated. Jensen wished she had the foresight to do it the day before it cost the life of a sailor. She shook her head knowing that hindsight had no equal; in looking back a person could solve all problems relating to yesterday without error.

The captain and the sailors returned to shore and readied their ship for the voyage home. With only three masts left and less than half their sails the trip to Sharks Way would take a week.

"We'll stop in Abithia on the way home," said Corel.

Jensen worried about her parents and brothers objected, "Why? We need to return and defeat the wizard."

"I need the sword of Kavar to defeat Kago his commander. He is protected by magic. The last time I fought him my sword hand outdid him but I was lucky to escape with my life. Twice I ran him through with my blade and twice I watched his wounds heal before my eyes," said Corel.

"I will take care of him," said Jensen.

"You will have concern enough with the wizard. He will busy you knowing your strength. I will be on my own with his ground forces," said Corel.

101

"He's right, the moment you enter the battlefield he will distract you from taking control of his men," said Katie.

"The sword of Kavar kills men whether magic protects or not. It was forged in the mines of the Keeper of the Dark," said Corel.

"Where is it now?" asked Jensen.

"In the hands of the Kanan the Dark, a highwayman who steals the lives and souls of men for the Keeper," said Corel.

"He rides at the full moon and takes all who are foolish enough to be out on that night," said Corel.

"How far away is Abithia?" asked Jensen.

"Three days," said Corel.

Jensen thought that the ship would be repaired and her knight might free the victims of Cambells Cross. That was not to be the case; they would go to Abithia and look for a special sword. They would only have one night during the month to accomplish this; the night of the full moon. She had no control over what was unfolding before her having to bend with the wishes of others. The lives of her parents and brothers rested in the hands of her allies and not only her own.

# THE GIFTED OF SISCERLY XVI
## *The Seer Escapes*

AT RAVENCROFT, KAMAHL'S CASTLE, Mira and Presela sat in his prison cell. The sun was starting to rise when the soldier guarding them dropped out of his chair to the ground. Mira's friend Mary came with a mace and a key to unlock the door.

"Julia was a friend of mine too and so are you. I'm going to Agnes's house and from there to the border another day. You two have to get out now or burn. Kamahl has decided he can't trust Presela anymore and doesn't want her to fall into enemy hands so will burn her too," said Mary.

"Thanks Mary. Let's go Presela," said Mira.

"What about mom?" asked Presela.

"She made her decision and let herself be seduced by Kamahl and his selfish cause. He has the power of persuasion in him and we can't fight that today. We have to get ourselves out or burn. Your mother will have to wait for another day. If we try to take her with us she'll give us away so let's go girl," said Mira.

They left by a secret way through alleys and hidden doors

that only the servants knew of. A closet in a corner of a kitchen had access to a tunnel used for the smuggling of wine and ale. Mary went to Agnes's house and Mira with Presela in hand went to the stables. Mira saddled Chimneysweep and they rode double out of town. They hoped no one would notice and no word had gotten around that they were enemies of Kamahl.

Mira and Presela rode from Kamahl's lands to the border between Ravenshire and Tyhton. Mira took the direct route hoping that no information of them would find its way there until after they were gone. The last to know anything of concern were the common soldiers, the ones that needed to know. It was the way of the world and who was Mira to scoff; she only knew the way things went. They were given little trouble as two women on one horse were of no consequence to sleepy border guards. The two countries were separated by a river with a bridge patrolled on both sides by the two countries.

Almost over the bridge a lightning bolt struck the ground ahead causing dirt and debris to fly high in the air. Mira raced Chimneysweep in a wild zigzag pattern along the river as lightning bolts struck close but missed. Mira knew it was only a matter of time before one hit them both so dumped Presela in the river where she would be safe.

"Stay in the water and hold Cromby's head high," screeched Mira.

Mira galloped along the river in a crazy zigzag pattern drawing fire away from Presela. The woods were not far and maybe she could hide from him in that dense growth.

Presela knew that unless she did something Mira would soon be hit. The witch was trying to make it to the woods but it was a long way off. Presela would send a message to Kamahl hoping to distract him.

"Kamahl it's me Presela, between me and Jensen we'll destroy you, I'm standing on the bridge. Can you see me right on the bridge," whispered Presela and hoped the message got through.

The lightning stopped and the orange glob spun in crazy circles. She moved close to the river bank and stayed low. Cromby shrieked in protest at being half submerged in the water; he wanted out.

"Kamahl it's me Presela I'm on the bridge can't you see me, on the bridge," whispered Presela.

The orb still spun then centred on Mira again and fired as she entered the woods. Mira galloped to the densest growth and halted, nothing came her way. Mira wondered why the wizard had stopped. She stayed for awhile then rode back toward the river checking the sky for the orb. Presela was sitting on the river bank, Cromby lying in the grass licking his fur.

"We got lucky. You all right?" asked Mira.

"Yes just wet."

The soldiers on the other side of the river now knew that the two were enemies of Kamahl so rushed to the bank opposite them and readied their bows. Mira waved her hands and chanted causing mist as thick as smoke to rise instantly around the archers blinding them. The arrows they fired went wild, nowhere close to the pair.

They quickly mounted and rode through the fields. Mira would stay away from the roads and take a back route to the castle. She didn't want to run into that glob again having no defence against the wizard's high magic.

Toward Siscerly they went Cromby in Presela's coat crouching low. In no time at all they arrived at the castle gates then to the palace where Nikita and Amie awaited. Mira felt shaky and in need of some medicinal comfort after the ordeal which almost cost her life. Mira would never be able to go to Ravencroft again or any other land governed by Kamahl. It was a big change in her life as she had been used to coming and going anywhere she pleased.

"I have to see some friends," said Mira and left.

Presela was given a room and introduced to her new life.

"What do I have to do here?" asked Presela.

"Only what you can and what you want. We force no one with a gift to do anything they deem immoral. We are gifted ourselves and know it is only freedom that makes that gift whole and gives us the full power to act. So do what you can to help us in our fight against Kamahl," said Amie.

Presela went to her room and searched for her mother's soul. She found it in the castle kitchen where she had been put to work to replace Mary who had strangely disappeared. Her mother was back where she started from, working for two coppers a day.

If her mother had just come along she would be in another palace by now. Presela worried about her but there was nothing she could presently do.

Presela did not fully understand but she'd heard the wizard's pitch herself. She'd seen it as a rouse but knew others would find peace in following his cause. Not everyone sought freedom as it required effort and risk; some felt safe within prison walls. Kamahl did give those that served him the feeling of safety with an unsaid promise of death if they betrayed or disappointed him. With no more than a stern look he could make a person's knees shake and a smile from him was all the reward most needed. He was certainly good at what he did; lead a country and that through war continued to expand its borders. An oppressor with a promise of security to all who bent to his will and death to those that dared to stand in his way.

The peace of following the oppressor instead of fighting him; a coward's way thought Presela. Someday she would go back and free her mother, but not today. Today she would stay and fight the wizard and his twisted ideals.

# THE GIFTED OF SISCERLY XVII
## *The Magic Sword*

JENSEN WATCHED AS THE sailors slowed to the port of Hagar then docked at the gateway to Abithia. Corel, Katie, and Jensen walked their mounts down the ramps toward the town. Here they would start their search for Kanan the Dark, a highwayman who stole lives and souls.

Jensen thought about her years at Cambells Cross and her family. Why did that wizard have to come along and change her simple life to this? She was being dragged by some force from one quest to another trying to put an end to her family's suffering, slaving in some mine. It was need that drove her but there seemed to be no end to the things she had to do, places she had to go to save her family and the villagers. Where was it all going to end?

They took the main road from town the night of a full moon; searching but found nothing, travelling one road then the next. The landscape was silver with long shadows and reminded Jensen of a winter night. There was even a chill in the air as though something was destined to happen. Owls hooted and wolves howled breaking an eerie stillness that hung in the air. Back and forth they rode the night long until the moon was high and bright as it would be.

The dark rider found them.

From the woods came a black horse, a shadowy figure sitting upon its back. The dark rider ran between them slashing at their heads with a large sword that glistened in the moonlight. Having failed at taking a single life he ran from them. Jensen chased the dark horse. Studs of metal stuck out from its halter and from the band about its chest; a menacing sight. A strange squealing sound came from the horse making it sound intimidating and eerie like a shrieking ghost. They followed the stallion pulling almost out of sight.

Jensen remembered what Amie had told her of Biscuit. The horse was from the land of the desert tribes to the south. The nomads of that tribe had bred horses for thousands of years aiming for speed and endurance. The little mare was a full hand shorter than most but Jensen had found her lacking in nothing to date. Her mount tended to fall asleep under normal travel and she was warned by Amie to push her a little every now and then.

She did just that.

Jensen pushed her heels into Biscuit's sides, the little mare responded as though knowing her duty was to catch the big black stallion ahead. They left Corel and Katie behind and narrowed the gap on the black stallion. Biscuit thundered down the road, little by little getting closer as the night wore on. The stallion dropped out of his gallop as the rider saw only her in pursuit. Kanan the Dark drew his sword and readied to take a soul.

Jensen was soon at his side, ducking his swings and

grasping his arm. The smell of rotting flesh made her gasp. Her grip on his forearm made his skin and flesh give way. Kanan was rotting: not dead yet not alive, one foot in this world, one in the next. Jensen's touch would have no affect on someone such as this. Jensen bent low as he swung at her with the great sword. She ducked his back swing then moved to his left out of the sword's reach. Katie and Corel were not yet in sight so she would have to find a way to slow him until they came.

"Claim my soul. It is worth a thousand others to the Keeper. I am an enchantress he seeks," said Jensen.

Jensen knew he must be wise to her value as Kanan followed swinging his sword at her. She galloped toward the woods seeking safety among the trees. She used Biscuit's shorter and stronger strides to her advantage over the long legged stallion. Kanan relentlessly followed swinging his sword as Biscuit dodged trees and jumped over logs in and effort to evade him. On and on they rode the black rider slashing and Jensen evading his swing. Tree limbs she ducked under, he broke through. Biscuit moved ever left keeping out of his reach.

Jensen came to steep hill before her and pushed Biscuit up the slope. The little mare responded by driving herself to the top, slipping on loose dirt as she went. The long legged stallion did not fare as well, his legs collapsing half way to the summit. The rider fell to the ground, the sword lost along the way. Jensen pushed her mount downhill to take advantage of his bad fortune.

Jensen scrambled toward the sword but Kanan's gloved hand clutched her throat. She groped for her dagger and found the hilt, grasped it and shoved the blade into his side. Kanan moved to her left in response and she slid from under him. Not even the magic of the dagger could stop him; it only slowed him slightly.

Jensen ran toward his sword and grasped it but was unable to lift much less wield the hefty blade. It was the only weapon that would send him on his final journey to the Underworld. Kanan staggered toward her, dagger in his side. With a deafening roar he lunged her way. Diving, holding both hands wide, he intended to snare her. Jensen jammed the hilt of the sword into the ground and pointed the tip upward, his way. Kana impaled himself on the blade roaring in pain.

Kanan refused to die, rose to his knees, and struggled to pull the long blade free. Jensen screamed in horror but found the strength to grasp his gloved hands and shove the sword even farther into his rotting frame. Smoke rose among the stench of burning flesh. Kanan roared and sank into the ground, half burning, half melting into the waiting Underworld below. Seconds later there remained only the imprint of a large man upon the parched ground.

Kanan's black stallion shrieked and ran Jensen's way as though the spirit of Kanan shifted to the horse. With a low blow to the big horse's legs Biscuit sent the black stallion sprawling. The black beast rose to his feet and shook himself. He stared at Biscuit and Jensen, shrieked in an ungodly tone. Seeing no affect on the two he slowly backed up then ran away.

Jensen sat head down sobbing as Katie hurried her way. Corel eyed the sword then claimed it as his own. Katie held Jensen close stroking her hair.

"It's over. Sorry I was so slow," said Katie.

Jensen rose to her feet and hugged Biscuit who in turn nuzzled her.

At dawn they left the black rider's imprint smoking in the

sun. They returned to port and loaded their mounts on board. The captain set sail toward Sharks Way, their last stop.

The sword that Jensen was unable to lift Corel wielded with ease. He flung it from left to right, over and under, with one hand or two. Jensen had seen many differences between that sword and others while struggling with the highwayman. It was distinct from others in detail and colour. The delicate craftsmanship of the hilt was not of this world. A metal replication of a snake wound it way to the blade in such detail as to make it look alive. The blade was dark blue in colour and did not reflect the morning sun.

Thoughts of the previous night haunted Jensen although she was trying to push it from her mind. The blade gleamed in the moonlight and was the reason she could duck the man's swing.

"There's something wrong with the sword," said Jensen.

"What?" said Katie.

Corel stopped swinging his new weapon and looked wide eyed her way.

"I saw the blade glimmer when in the hands of the Highwayman. It's dull now, no shine at all," said Jensen.

"It's the Keeper's work. It probably reflects only moonlight," said Katie.

"Maybe. I still feel something is wrong."

"It's the right sword. There's no other like it," said Katie.

Jensen was developing a sense for magic; she thought about it a lot lately knowing small details might save her life one day. She was troubled about the sword, the dull look of it. She watched Corel wipe the snake hilt and blade as though trying to bring lustre to his new acquisition but it looked the same as before. She remembered handling the sword herself; remembered it gleam in her hands.

"May I hold it?" asked Jensen.

"Sure," said Corel.

He stuck the point of the weapon into the deck, hilt in the air. Jensen grasped the sword and it immediately shone bright blue.

"What does it mean?" asked Corel.

"I don't know," said Jensen.

"You killed the Highwayman so maybe that's the way the magic of it works," said Katie.

Jensen didn't even try to pull the weapon from the deck and as she released her grip on it the sword lost its brightness. She left the weapon and a confused Corel behind and walked to the bow, Katie close. Something else worried her and those thoughts refused to let he be.

"Katie, do you think the Keeper can trace the sword and know where the owner is?"

"I don't think so."

"If he knows where we are can he send another storm?"

"No. He rules only his realm and is powerless in this one, unless of course Kamahl gets his way."

The winds were fair, as a matter of fact perfect according to the captain. The direction was also ideal to get them home in the shortest possible time.

"Do you think things are all of a sudden going too good? Maybe we're headed into another trap," said Jensen.

"Oh, cheer up; we're bound to have a little good luck now and then. Enjoy it," said Katie.

"Corel doesn't say much to me. I think he tries to avoid me. Why's that?" asked Jensen.

Jensen was hurt by his silence and he obviously avoided her. "He's a man's man. He's afraid of your power. You can bend him around your finger if you wanted to. It's the first time he's had to live with that thought. Give him time," said Katie.

Jensen liked Corel and was distraught that her power worked against getting to know the man. Being gifted had so far yielded her few friends and many enemies. Looking at Katie though she had to admit that the few friends she had were worth a lot.

# THE GIFTED OF SISCERLY XVIII
## *A Dangerous Dragon*

At Ravencroft Kamahl sat in his study knowing that he needed a Seer especially since Nikita now had one, his, stolen from him a week ago. He just happened to have one in his prison. A High Priestess as a matter of fact, but she had refused to do anything for him even under threat of death. She ruled the first land he had captured after becoming king. Kamahl had her summoned and would try to reason with the priestess one more time.

"Welcome dear Ises, I hope things are well with you and your accommodations are adequate. I'll get right to the point. I need a Seer as I seem to have lost mine. So I've decided to give you a chance," said Kamahl.

"And I refuse," said Ises.

"In the last week I've had two thousand of your countrymen brought to my dungeons where they have renounced their faith and then put to death. Their souls were traded to the Lord of the Underworld himself for certain favours. If you refuse I will do the same to two thousand more this week and so on. Do you understand?" asked Kamahl.

"Yes, I will do as you say but my power is weak here. I can only see from the place where I was captured, the Isle of the Gods."

"Then that is where you will go with one of my commanders and do whatever you do to bring me some news of what Nikita is doing," said Kamahl.

"If I hear you've executed more of my people then you get nothing," said Ises.

"Soldiers take her to the Isle, commander stay here a moment if you will," said Kamahl.

They both watched Ises leave the room.

"I wanted to tell you this after she's left. Don't trust her in the least, she devious and clever. Her servant Nara is true to me so get information from her frequently to see what the priestess is up to. She only has power on that island so there's really nowhere for her to go. I do need a Seer so that's why I'm taking a chance but if she threatens me in anyway don't hesitate to execute her. Go now and keep me posted," said Kamahl.

Ises knew that Kamahl would need another Seer after the loss of Presela so he would be sending for her shortly. She could not do anything from her prison cell but might be able to from her isle. Ises accepted with just enough resistance to make him think she was fighting the idea when actually she wanted to go. As for Nara, what did Kamahl think a Seer did anyway? The little tramp was working for him and so what. She would use her to deceive Kamahl.

Ises believed that men like Kamahl usually built many enemies and that would sooner or later be his downfall. She could not foresee his death but felt that it lay in the near future, or maybe it was just a hope. She would try her best to hasten the event.

Presela sat on her bed petting Cromby then went numb at the visions in her mind. It was a huge dark form the size of a house: it had four legs, a head the size of a man with dagger like teeth, and a long tail with spikes. Its body was covered with lizard like scales and more spikes ran down its long neck. It breathed fire. What on earth could do that? Presela heard stories of Dragons but never believed they were real yet seldom had visions that were false. She rushed from the room to see Amie for advice then heard loud roars from the street.

Presela ran as fast as she could to the street and saw the beast through Cromby's eyes. Her vision came too late. The dragon was destroying the market and killing people, setting all aflame. Soldiers rushed toward it with spears but were brushed aside like dead leaves. Its claws ripped through bodies and its jaws through steel as soldier's armour crumpled under attack from the deadly beast.

Nikita rushed to battle the dragon, "Presela try to read its mind," she yelled as her hands went high in the air.

Nikita's hands pushed forward as she chanted words Presela could not understand. The beast was driven backward and tumbled twice then stood on its hind legs. It looked at the sorceress with blank eyes. Nikita and the beast were locked in a stare neither making a move.

"Darrow. Why are you doing this?" yelled Presela.

The beast looked toward Presela, his big eyes growing in size.

"You're not evil so leave us alone," yelled Presela again.

The beast opened his transparent wings and slowly took flight.

"The Dragons have never bothered us before. What did you see in his mind?" asked Nikita.

"I saw rage at first but then when you tossed him backward his mind changed, as if he awoke. He was stunned and did not understand. I know his name is Darrow that's about all, and Nikita I could feel the wizard's presence in him. It's like a smell of a perfume, a scent on someone, you know if they were there. Well I can do the same with my gift, I can feel he was within Darrow's mind recently," said Presela.

"That's all we need now, a crazy Dragon roaming the countryside destroying villages and killing my soldiers. Could you find him if you had to?" asked Nikita.

"Yes, I think I could. I know where he is now at least."

Nikita surveyed the damage and dispatched help where it was needed. Presela did what she could to console wounded and crying families of the dead. She looked at the destruction that beast had caused and wondered what was next.

# THE GIFTED OF SISCERLY XIX
## *The Woman Warrior*

THE SHIP DOCKED AT Sharks Way, Jensen glad to be standing on solid ground. She felt heavier and stomped her feet into the earth as though confirming it was real. They took their horses to the stable paying for grooming as well as hay and oats. Jensen turned Biscuit loose in the big paddock for exercise after four days aboard ship. The little mare kicked her heels in the air and ran about aimlessly. Biscuit found a mud hole and rolled back and forth over it enjoying whatever horses enjoy when doing so. Jensen laughed but knew she would have to give the stable boy an extra coin for the work he had ahead.

Jensen left the barn in time to see Katie, Corel, and Shaun walking toward the inn, Katie in the lead. Jensen was in no mood for drunken men and their lack of manners so decided to go to Katie's cabin and rest. She walked toward the edge of town looking over her shoulder often as she went.

Jensen felt eyes upon her and saw residents peering at her from windows along the street. It wasn't them; it was something evil that was making her tremble and feel ill. Her awareness was increasing day by day as her power grew stronger. She felt all her senses were being affected by the gift.

Something was stalking her.

The door to Katie's cabin was in the rear so went there but hid in the nearby woods and watched the door from the cover of bushes. Moments later a tall woman wearing a dark cape went to the door and knocked. When no one answered she peaked through a window then returned to the door and tested the latch. The woman kicked at the door causing it to spring open.

The big woman carefully stepped inside and soon returned looking into the forest. Jensen ducked low as her gaze passed then peered through the gaps in the leaves. The woman bent and examined tracks around the back of the cabin. Too many footsteps on the earth this close to town would leave her no trail to follow. She seemed reluctant to leave but finally did so.

Jensen dared not move until she was long gone then snuck deeper into the woods fearing the big woman may lay in wait. Jensen knew she'd been spotted and the woman would not give up easily. She sensed that woman had been sent by the wizard; a woman as Jensen had no power over her; another assassin.

Jensen found a deer path and followed it through the dense woods. She was careful not to leave a trail, stepping on rocks or patches of grass, also taking care not to leave a trail of broken twigs. Movement ahead caused her to hide in bushes not far from the path. As she peered trough gaps in her leafy cover the woman walked into view not making a sound. It was the big woman without her cape, her black hair tied back in a ponytail. The woman warrior was muscled as a man with arms and shoulders bigger than most. The warrior was scantly dressed in black leather a short sword on her left hip, a dagger on her right, and a small battleaxe tied behind the dagger. She looked for broken twigs, any sign of someone passing. Jensen was glad about the extra care she had taken.

The woman moved along the trail, Jensen not far behind. Jensen was not following in pursuit but thought it wise keeping the warrior in sight instead of wondering where she was. Jensen took great care as she suspected the woman knew how to use her weapons and didn't just carry them for show. The woman would occasionally turn and scan the forest. Jensen never stuck her head in the air, only watched her from between leaves on boughs.

The assassin was almost back at the cabin and stopped, crouching low as if stalking. Jensen strained to see what the warrior was looking at then saw Katie walking around the back of the cabin. Katie was alone and probably returned to keep her company. The woman pulled the battleaxe from her belt and crept closer. The wizard must be after all or the woman seeing red hair assumed it was Jensen. Something had to be done; she couldn't let Katie die.

Jensen moved as swiftly and lightly as possible hoping the woman would occupy herself with Katie and not be aware of her attack. Jensen saw Katie eyeing the broken door and removing her belt, shaking it nervously and looking around. The assassin stopped then must have heard Jensen's last step. She turned to see Jensen only half hidden. The warrior woman was coming her way.

"Katie look out there's an assassin in here. She's after me now," yelled Jensen.

"Hold on. I'm coming," yelled Katie.

The woman was still out of striking range but raised her

arm throwing the battleaxe at Jensen. Jensen saw a blur flying her way so moved to avoid it. The blade passed her right arm cutting her flesh as it flew by.

Katie walked toward the assassin sword in hand, murder in her eyes. The assassin turned to meet Katie drawing her own sword and holding it high. Katie was just barely out of striking range as she pushed her sword toward the woman hard enough to deal a lethal blow. Jensen did not understand the meaning of the gesture as the point of the sword would stop short. Jensen watched in awe as the sword turned into a long spear and pierced the warrior woman's chest. The assassin dropped to the ground, dead.

"Wow, I owe you for that one," said Jensen.

Katie approached and seeing the blood on her arm looked to her, "That was a warrior of the Koto-Ri. They poison the blades of their weapons. We have to get you back to the castle, now."

Jensen walked at Katie's side her friend tying the snake belt around her waist. They walked to the stable and saddled their horses. Corel and Shaun were on their way out of the inn.

"Jensen's been cut by the blade of a Koto-Ri. We're going back to the castle," yelled Katie.

Jensen was starting to feel the affect of something within, growing tired but still able to ride. She pushed Biscuit, the little horse responding as though sensing something not right with Jensen. The mare's strides lengthened and quickened; she saw Katie dropping behind. Jensen had to get back before she passed out. If she didn't make it her friend was close behind and would help her. The road grew blurry and darker. She could not feel her limbs and gripped the saddle tight but felt nothing. The wind in her face making her eyes water told her that Biscuit was still at full speed.

Jensen could not judge time as she slipped in and out of awareness. She did not want Biscuit to kill herself but was unable to pull back the reins to slow her. She briefly saw what looked like the castle gates as Biscuit thundered through to the cobblestone yard. Visions of people running out of her way and the sound of hooves echoing from the walls filled her mind. The mare approached what looked like the Princess's Palace and as a man exited Biscuit raced in.

It could not be thought Jensen; it must be a dream brought on by the poison. The horse was now running up the stone steps, people moving aside. Jensen clung to the saddle not believing her cloudy vision as they entered the rooms of the Princess herself. Biscuit sunk to her knees and Jensen fell off her back. Jensen strained to look at the mare lying on the floor beside her. She looked up at Amie's face then her world went black.

Jensen saw her parents and her teasing brothers, saw them as they played board games after supper. Jensen laughed as she caught Colby the oldest cheating, screamed when Jarrod pulled her hair. Her parents were always hugging and holding each other. She watched as aunt Susan came to visit with Uncle Dave in tow. Then she saw the soldiers take everyone away. Jensen saw the wizard's lightning and visions of alligators, snakes, and spiders as they filled her mind. They all closed in, the lightning, a snake coiled around her, and an alligator closed its jaws on her arm. Jensen screamed and for a second saw a face she knew, Katie.

Jensen felt herself move from Cambells Cross to the swamps and then the angry sea. Over and over the cycle repeated from happiness to fear and hate. Jensen felt a hand on hers and thought she saw the face of her friend again, Katie. She saw the face of a man his skin and hair grey, the colour of death. He was tall with broad shoulders, neither thin nor fat. The man's eyes were also grey but stood out from the rest of him as he stared. The grey man looked at her with contempt; the look of someone who had caught her stealing. He raised his arm and threw a lightning bolt her way. Jensen ducked; the wizard was in her dreams, had somehow entered her mind. Jensen screamed and ran but wherever she went he was there before her.

Jensen gasped then saw a blinding light; it hurt her eyes and made her head ache. She closed them and opened them slowly. Katie's face was before her.

"You're back with us," said Katie, a smile graced her face.

"How long?" said Jensen her throat felt like desert sand.

"Take some water, here. You were out almost a week."

"Biscuit?"

"Oh she's like you, resting. She saved your life. Took you right to Amie. Up ten flights of stairs. Right into the Princess's stateroom then passed out."

Jensen tried to laugh then drank more water.

"She's still there. They couldn't carry her down the stairs so they're waiting until she's well enough to walk herself. The cleaning staff has to bring hay and water ten flights up and carry horse dung down," said Katie.

"How did she know where to go?"

"Probably followed Amie's scent. Until you came Biscuit used to be her horse."

"She gave me her horse?"

"Yah a special horse I'd say."

"The Princess must be upset," said Jensen getting her voice back.

"What Niki? No she likes the company, goes out and pets her quite a bit."

"Niki?"

"Yah, Nikita the Princess."

"You're friends?"

"Oh yes. I've known her as long as I can remember."

"I'm hungry, no, I'm more than hungry."

"Food coming up."

Jensen watched as Katie left the room to find her something to eat. Amie came in a couple of minutes later.

"Good to see you better child."

"How long has Katie been here?" asked Jensen.

"She never left, was always by your side."

"I thought she was. She called the woman a Koto-Ri?"

"The warriors of the Koto-Ri are mercenaries. They're assassins for hire. Simple thugs who will do anything for a price. They are good at what they do though, I'll give them that. I think Kamahl will have more than one out hunting for you."

Princess Nikita entered the room.

"How are you feeling?"

"Better your Princess Nikita," said Jensen unsure how to formally address her.

"Call me Niki, all my friends do. Thanks for bringing Corel home."

Jensen could never imagine calling the Princess Niki.

"He's not an easy man to find."

"Ha we know," said Amie.

Katie entered the room followed by kitchen staff.

"Well, we'll let you eat and come and see you later," said Niki.

Katie pushed a table over to the bed.

"I'm joining you; I haven't had much to eat either."

"Did Corel ask about me?"

"Everybody has asked."

Jensen wasn't interested in everybody else; she was only concerned as to whether Corel had been asking about her. She didn't care if she was one of many that loved him as long as she was one.

Jensen was able to do more day by day, finally able to ride. Biscuit was ready to run so that's what they did.

# The Gifted of Siscerly XX
### *The Power of Ises*

Amie and Niki went through the old books of magic written by wizards hundreds and even thousands of years before. They were looking for information on enchantresses and that rare gift of theirs. They were fewer than witches or sorceresses having that rare gift of both magic and charm. A charm no man could deny and magic in their touch.

Listen to this Amie, "Monamy an enchantress two thousand years ago set the city of Adema aflame with the wave of her hand. She moved soldiers out of her way without a touch and lifted an enemy off the ground pushing him back against a wall. She had the same power as a wizard as well as control over men."

"Do they say how she performed these feats?" said Amie.

"She used Ki Ru Oka and chants of those beliefs," said Niki.

"Not a subtle form. I think it a little too abrupt for Jensen," said Amie.

"All right then listen to this. Shana Ram was the first

enchantress three thousand years ago and was a follower of Capernious. She had a full power as well," said Niki.

"Did she have power over women though?" asked Amie.

"I don't know. It only says they feared her one and all," said Niki.

"We have to find a way to give Jensen the power to deal with women sent her way. She's a light woman and will never be able to battle the way Katie can. She's defenceless against most women that comes her way," said Amie.

"Oh listen to this. Chinela the last enchantress could shock the body of a man, woman, or beast with her touch. They would be rendered unconscious or die," said Niki.

"How did she accomplish it?" asked Amie.

"A wizard made her a bracelet that transformed her enchantress power into the power of shock. They said like an eel in the sea," said Niki.

"Can you make one for her?" asked Amie.

"I can try. It will take a while and lots of experimenting but yes, I can try," said Niki.

They both went to the goldsmith and gave him instructions on what they wanted him to make.

Ises had seen Presela while imprisoned at Ravencroft and had felt the woman's mind while passing in a hallway, the mind of another Seer. Like a unique face and look everyone has their own distinct aura or ambience and those with the gift can distinguish one from the other sometimes half a world apart. Ises did not know exactly how her gift worked or why. Only that it did and how to use it. As with any other talent it took practise, patience, and most of all belief to become proficient in its use.

Ises kneeled in the temple on the Isle of the Gods, a place where her power was peak. In Ravencroft she could not read Kamahl's thoughts. He could not only block her but also cause great pain if she dared to try. On the island Ises could read Kamahl's every thought, unknown to him. He was a wizard with many talents, a jack of all trades. Ises was a master of only one, a Seer.

Today however Ises was not reading Kamahl, she was scanning the mind of the commander out in the yard assigned the task of a jailer.

He hated his job; hated the temple, and the quiet.

He was looking for any excuse he could find to kill the priestess and return to the castle, away from this isolation. The only women here were off limits and not to be touched by order of Kamahl himself. The commander hated that and was used to taking whatever he wanted in countries they had conquered. It was the reward for risking his life in battle. He took his share of the booty. He found it frustrating seeing these beautiful priestesses walking in sheer robes and not being able to lay just claim to them.

Ises could read his every thought and knew that she would not die of old age with him around. The commander was a walking bundle of nerves ready to break. Ises would have to kill him. His second in command would take over; a young man she knew and could handle. If the commander died no questions would be asked. Everyone would be content moving up a notch in the world. That's what priestesses did; they found ways to make their followers happy.

When they took her the first time she was at the head of her army, the one that Kamahl destroyed. She surrendered with five thousand soldiers still alive; Ises could not let them all die.

Kamahl beheaded all five thousand men who had submitted to him to set an example to monarchs of other countries that had the tenacity to fight him.

Ises was guilty of mass stupidity for surrendering to him. Ises should have been able to see it coming and maybe did but hoped for the best.

Ises picked up the amulet, the ones given to the High Priestess in the name of the Gods. No one knew where it came from but everyone suspected it was the gift from the Goddess, Assyla. It gave one the power to be invisible to most. Ises wished she had had it when imprisoned by Kamahl. He would be dead by now.

Ises drew the dagger, the one forged by the Gods and dropped from the heavens for the High Priestess to use. It would kill anything that walked the earth; it would even kill that half demon, half human Kamahl.

She touched the amulet and looked at herself in the mirror. Her reflection was not there. She held the dagger tight and went to the yard to visit the nervous commander and say good bye.

# THE GIFTED OF SISCERLY XXI
## *The Hunt for a Dragon*

THE SUN BURNED HOT high above the horizon in an empty sky melting the morning mist from the castle for another day. Jensen and Biscuit had been out getting a little fresh air and exercise. Jensen rode in through the front gate past the fountain where a flock of sparrows took a morning bath. Shop keepers set in place their wares and were already bickering over prices with early shoppers. Children played with sticks and balls on side streets always empty until the evening hours.

Stone masons and carpenters toiled rebuilding the market burned to the ground by an angry dragon two weeks ago. It had happened only two days before Jensen's return from an overseas voyage in search of a knight. Bedridden after her body was filled with poison from the tainted blade of a female warrior, she had not been aware of the destruction until two days ago. Jensen had never seen a dragon but the thought of seeing one stirred her as nothing before. A beast as big as a house that breathed fire and flew; the idea filled her with awe more than fear. It was something to be avoided yet had to be seen. They were two emotions that battled within the human soul.

At the stable the smell of fresh bedding and hay filled the air. On entering Jensen noticed Nikita and Presela loading a pack horse and making preparations for a journey.

"Where are you going?" asked Jensen.

"To find the dragon, Darrow, and stop him from doing any more harm," said Nikita.

"How are you going to find it?" asked Jensen.

"Presela is a Seer. She can also feel life forces. She may be able to find this one too," said Nikita.

"Well if that's the case then I'm going along," demanded Jensen.

"You're just out of bed. You almost died," said Nikita.

"Almost, but I'm all right now and I'm going along and Katie is too so wait for us a few minutes, all right?"

Jensen did not want to miss this opportunity hoping to somehow make the dragon an ally. His name was Darrow and he was a male so maybe her gift would work on him. She had to try. With a dragon to aid her she would have a better chance at getting to Kamahl. Jensen ran into the castle to find Katie then both returned, packed and ready to go.

Jensen stared at the four sapphire rings Niki wore, two on the middle fingers of each hand. Katie had told her of rings and tokens worn by sorceresses and witches. They were stores of energy that could be called upon when needed to cast spells or otherwise boost their strength. The sun was the source of power stored in the rings being charged by the light of day.

Jensen watched Niki reach into the pocket of her ridding trousers and pulled out a fifth ring.

"Here Jensen, this is for you. It's a storage ring and I've

infused it with magic especially tailored for you. To turn it on just say Raj Mituck and to shut it off say Raj Katan."

"I don't know how to thank you for this, no, it's too much, I can't take it."

"Then borrow it for awhile. Until you earn it and believe me if you're around me for long, earn it you will," said Niki.

Jensen looked down at the ring which fit nicely on the large middle finger of her right hand. It shone greenish blue depending on how the light struck it. The sapphire was as large as the end of her thumb and would take a normal family's life savings to buy.

They rode down the street and out the front gate.

"It's not easy to use these rings and it will take a little practice so don't count on it. Don't stake your life on it until you find out whether it works for you or not, all right?" said Katie.

"Yah, Raj Mituck, hey I felt something in my hand when I said that and I'm starting to feel funny, stronger," said Jensen.

"It doesn't charge you Jensen, it only gives power to your gift, so don't get excited yet," said Niki with a smile.

"I can hardly wait to try it out," said Jensen.

Jensen could not go any longer than four of Biscuit's strides without looking down at the ring. Never in her life did she dream of wearing a ring such as this. Jensen looked at Katie who was smiling at her then peeked back at Niki who was wearing a rare grin directed Jensen's way. Presela also had a smile over her otherwise blank look and the cat was surely laughing at her too. They think I'm nuts over the ring and I guess I am thought Jensen.

They were heading northwest to skirt left of Kamahl's troops as they occupied the north. Kamahl had not taken a strip of land along the coast because it was considered holy land. Not that Kamahl would care but his soldiers feared that ancient city and would desert if stationed near those statues of dead men and ruined temples.

The sun sat on the highest mountain peak maintaining a delicate balance while it flooded the foothills with red light making all appear to be ablaze. A cool breeze blew out of the hills fanning through the tall dry grass which streamed like seas of fire. The trees cast long shadows hiding predators within readying for the night hunt. Jensen gathered wood for the fire as Katie sat rubbing her feet. Niki was looking intently at maps and Presela opened bags of food and leather packs containing pots, plates, and spoons.

"Where to now?" asked Katie.

"We keep going northwest along the coast and when we clear Kamahl's lands we go northeast, probably to the Eigelhorn Ridge which is what we run into in two days time. It makes sense that the dragon would live in those mountains honeycombed with caves," said Niki.

"And land of the dwarfs," said Katie.

"That too, so we had better take care they are rather malevolent at times," said Niki.

"What are the dwarfs?" asked Jensen.

"Short stocky beings the tallest coming to about the height of your chest," said Niki.

"And mean as rattle snakes," said Katie.

"Like I said we'll have to take care," said Niki.

Niki was in the process of cooking and Presela helped. They were assembling a full three course meal over a campfire. After the meal Niki and Presela cleaned up; they were the first to finish and eager to do so.

"Don't get used to the dessert, the cream will be sour by tomorrow," said Presela.

After dinner they sat around the campfire and watched a fountain of amber flames billow and swirl when Niki tossed a dry branch on the dying embers.

Jensen was eyeing her ring again as it changed colours in the varying light.

"Raj Mituck," Jensen whispered and everyone laughed. She knew that she would be the focus of more jokes to come so let her mind settle in for the duration. If they only understood what it meant for a girl from Cambells Cross to wear a ring such as this.

"Does Kamahl get his power from rings?" asked Jensen.

"I don't know where his power comes from. I tried to find out before I left but never did. He has a tremendous amount though as the things he does from a great distance require great reserves of energy," said Presela.

"If we knew then we could destroy it and he'd be helpless," said Niki.

"What if he gets it from the dark side, how do we destroy that?" asked Jensen.

Jensen looked at Presela and Cromby as the seer stroked the cat. Presela was a pretty girl but Jensen could never get used to the blank look that always set upon her face. Jensen could never read her; she never showed fear or any other emotion except the occasional smile. And that smile made it look as though Presela knew it all. Oh well, they were both on the same side so let it be thought Jensen. That blank look must have something to do with working and living so close to

Kamahl for a long time. Being in the castle with the Wizard of Death would probably put a solemn look on anyone's face.

Jensen was occasionally set back by some of Presela's insights and visions as well; the seer had knowledge of people beyond what she told or so Jensen suspected. It was eerie sometimes being near one with a gift like hers. How far could she see into your soul? Jensen felt naked some nights thinking her personal thoughts then looking up into Presela's seeing all face staring at her through those dead eyes.

They would be lost without her this trip. How would they know which way to go without Presela's gift to light the way?

"I make you nervous don't I Jensen. I'm sorry but I'm just who I am," said Presela.

"No, No, I get spooked at everything on days like this, it's not you, just me," said Jensen.

Oh, she did it again thought Jensen. She knew everything I thought. Then she saw a wry smile on Presela's lips and wondered if she had just been fooled.

"Let's get some sleep, we'll talk more tomorrow on the trail, I'll take first watch," said Niki.

Jensen lay looking up at the fading moon as it glowed behind transparent clouds. Few stars would make an appearance tonight as the world lay in decision as to whether or not it should rain. A slight breeze wafted through the trees while crickets and bullfrogs sounded all around. Jensen remembered nothing else until she was shaken and awoke.

"Your watch," whispered Niki.

Jensen hated second watch as she would have to fall asleep twice. That was probably why Niki had taken the first. She decided to leave last watch for Presela as it would be the easiest on the blind girl. Imagine that, a blind girl taking a watch.

Presela had insisted though saying she had superior sight looking through Cromby's eyes; the eyes of a night predator. Besides being spooked by her gift at times Jensen liked the girl; the seer wanted no favours and did more than her share. She never apologized when making a mistake misjudging something looking through her cat's eyes. Presela never drew attention to her disability.

The sight of Presela and Niki riding together in the light of the midday sun still burned in Jensen's mind. She could not get over how white Presela's hair was; as white as her fully white eyes. Niki's hair was blonde and shone gold in the bright sun like a crown around her beautiful face. She was a princess and it was as though nature had given her the look of one to accompany her role. Niki's life force blazed like a thousand candles. Her looks and status matched so thoroughly that it could not have been a coincidence; magic must have been involved thought Jensen, yah magic. What else could it be?

Besides her stunning looks Niki had an element of danger about her. She had a commanding presence even greater than her physical beauty. People tended to lose their nerve around her and fell silent giving her an edge with most. Even people that didn't know her lost their voice when she approached. Niki was definitely suited to running a country, especially one under siege.

Jensen woke Katie for her watch then managed somehow to fall asleep. She was awakened by Presela and Cromby before the light of day. Jensen was about to protest but then noticed a thin horizontal strip of orange light creep over the horizon under wisps of scattered clouds; something only a cat would see. Daylight slowly spread across the land giving colour where recently it was only purple and black.

All was quiet as they saddled and packed. They mounted and followed the coast road close to an angry morning sea. The rest of the day alternated between sun and clouds; rain threatened but never came.

That evening they reached the Temples of the Sun and Jensen knew why seasoned soldiers cowered from the sight. The statues and towers were gray and black from age and effects of the sea. They stood like black swords thrust from the bowels of the earth. Gaps in the clouds allowed pale bars of light to strike the ground around the buildings and stone images of dead men adding an ominous appearance to the scene. Biscuit backed away in fear of what she saw and felt. Animal instinct drove the horse away from the sight. Jensen would have urged her mount to run if it were not for the fact she rode between a sorceress, a witch, and a seer of the dark. Jensen was definitely safe as one could be amongst buried demons and shades.

"We'll camp here for the night," said Niki.

Jensen's heart almost stopped.

Night and darkness came too soon for Jensen as she looked over her shoulder often. Katie smiled in assurance more than once that evening but Jensen did not believe that confident look on her friend's face. Jensen knew something was coming for them even if the others did not.

"I'll take first watch," said Jensen a little too loud and no one protested her claim. They all stared at her, startled, their eyes wide.

"Is everything all right Jensen?" asked Niki.

"Yah, all is good but don't you feel danger here?"

"No, sorry I don't but if you know something we don't then tell us please," said Niki.

Jensen thought to herself that it's all right for a sorceress powerful as she to look down on mortals like herself.

"No, nothing just a feeling like the world is not on my side today," said Jensen.

"We all feel like that sometimes," said Niki.

Jensen only nodded then looked at Presela; blind and without resource other than her own will and not afraid. The others rolled up and slept leaving Jensen with the spirits and the dark. The remnants of the fire cast a dim light in the immediate area in contrast to the blackness that surrounded her. Sitting at the campfire within the expanse of darkness she felt like a single firefly in the dead of night; vulnerable and a target for anything wishing to do harm.

The stillness of night, the lack of wind did not settle her in the least. Jensen heard the slithered scraping sound like someone drawing a blade. It could be anything she told herself but then again it could be someone drawing a blade. Her heart contracted into a painful knot as she searched the darkness for any hint of motion. Jensen was afraid to look behind from where the sound came but slowly did and was relieved when nothing looked back. The atmosphere of the place made her jittery leaving only raw nerves that twitched at the slightest sounds. With a lump in her throat and a bruised heart she finished her watch. Katie relieved her with a kiss on the cheek.

"Go to sleep little one. I fear you've been chilled by the night. Sometimes things we can't see are worse than the ones we can."

Jensen fell asleep as Katie stroked her arm and sat beside her unwilling to leave. Her best friend in the world always by her side, Jensen loved that woman more than anyone could ever know.

# THE GIFTED OF SISCERLY XXII
## *The Dwarfs*

THE SUN APPEARED ABOVE the horizon painting the sky and giving colour to the trees and the ground. The fading moon glowed dimly behind scattered transparent clouds and birds sang to those awake. Dew drops on the leaves shone like diamonds in the light of the morning sun. Jensen yawned and stretched feeling hungry after her emotions the night before. She scraped her plate and licked her spoon finishing every morsel there was to eat.

Jensen quickly saddled Biscuit wanting to leave this ruined world of crumbling statues and temples behind. She felt like a thief stealing away with her life still intact.

The jagged peaks ahead raised high into the sky threatening and bold. Jensen was well ahead of the others when she stopped to look at the dead man's head jammed on a pole. It stood erect the height of a normal man its eyes open wide in fright. Things just kept getting better all the time. The third day out and they had not encountered another soul except this poor man. He could not speak yet told volumes of the world he lived in; it was not the place to make a mistake. The others caught up as Jensen scanned the horizon for signs of his executioners. They were not people she wanted to meet.

"There are northern tribes that wander the forests. He was probably a traveller or hunter that offended them in some way. They eat all but the head," said Katie.

"Oh come on, your putting me on right, right Katie?" said Jensen.

Jensen looked to Katie as she rode on without saying a word, a wry smile on her face. She never knew when the witch was telling the truth.

That afternoon Jensen rode ahead again and found out it was surely a mistake. She was confronted by a lone warrior dressed in animal skins and carrying a spear. She stopped Biscuit and did not even attempt to pass only looking into the forest for others to come her way.

"Good day sir," said Jensen.

The man with the spear was silent and did not shift his stare. Tall and muscular he would have been intimidating to others but to Jensen was merely another man. His wife if he had one would be more of a threat to her. She decided however to do nothing until the others came wondering if he was on his own. The others rode into the scene and before any conversation could be shared ten more of his kind appeared from behind trees and closed around them spears threatening, held high.

Jensen knew that if Niki did anything a lot of these warriors would die. Niki's gift was not a subtle art; her explosive power at times was hard for her to precisely control. Jensen looked at Niki who gave her the nod; Jensen's exacting power over men would be used.

"Raj Mituck," said Jensen and the sapphire on her ring started to glow. Jensen dismounted and stared into their eyes with a look that said back off and let me be. Looking at each one for only seconds she felt her power flow. From her eyes to theirs she saw light and felt the surge.

"Go from here and let us pass we mean you no harm," she said.

One by one Jensen looked into their eyes and spears lowered. Then with a nod they left without saying a word.

Jensen looked down at the stone still gleaming blue.

"Raj Katan," she said and it immediately glowed green.

"It worked Niki, I don't feel weak at all," said Jensen.

"That's good we may have further need of it shortly," said Niki.

They rode north until the granite walls of the mountain blocked their way.

"Well, we only have two choices, east or west which one will it be?" said Katie.

Presela looked west and said, "We'll camp here and in the morning go west. I can feel it strongest in that direction but I am slightly confused. The life force I feel is not quite the same, it seems different somehow."

"We have nothing else to go on so west it shall be," said Niki.

As Jensen unsaddled Biscuit she thought about how well they all worked together under Niki's lead.

They started the campfire before sundown and finished their meals before dark. That evening they all had a lot to say and the whole night to chat. They shared wine that Niki had stashed away for a special occasion.

"This is not really a special occasion but we did get here

and that's a start. We can't be far from the dragon now and may have to battle him tomorrow so let's drink to that," said Niki.

Jensen took last watch that night and was the first to hear Cromby hiss. Presela woke and held her cat tight as it scanned the bushes and trees. Jensen squinted into the forest but saw nothing. She continued to search for movement and listened for sounds of anything that didn't belong. A heavy silence engulfed them as they all stood waiting for something to happen. Cromby was never wrong.

"We're surrounded. There's about a hundred or so well back in the woods," said Presela.

Jensen did not doubt her in the least but wondered how she could miss an army of a hundred men. She still saw nothing.

"All right we'll continue on as normal and see what they do. Can you tell if they're dwarfs?" said Niki.

"I can't tell there's nothing to compare their height to except trees," said Presela.

That morning they loaded the packhorse and saddled the others while shooting glances toward the trees. Jensen felt she was being watched, her hair almost stood straight at the back of her head. She still saw nothing, not a sign or a sound of what made her feel tense and ready to flee. Biscuit and the other horses also knew something was there as they snorted and stiffened ready to run.

Before Jensen could mount Biscuit a little man came from the woods standing straight and proud but not tall. He was well dressed and looked clean but the thing that stood out most of all was the large hammer stuck into his belt at his right and the war axe on his left. He walked close looking up with no fear in his eyes at all.

"You will come with me," he said, definitely meant as an order and not a request.

Jensen looked at Niki and saw the others doing the same. Niki looked down at the little man a slight scowl on her face. The dwarf raised his hand and whistled. In seconds a hundred more came from the trees. The horses snorted and were hard to control as everyone fought at the reins.

"I will rephrase. You will come with us," said the little man with a smile on his face.

Jensen felt great discomfort as Niki stood like a stone statue glaring at him. She knew Niki didn't like being threatened. The little man did not know who he was pushing or that smile would not be on his face. Jensen fingered her ring ready to release its power then noticed Katie's hand on her snake belt waiting to do the same. Niki sighed then rolled her eyes acting as though she were merely being inconvenienced.

"All right let's go with him, I can never refuse an invitation," said Niki.

The little man lost his smile after being patronized but did nothing else only pointed the way. They moved west along the mountain wall, their horses calm and Cromby was quiet. Over a stream and into a mountain cave they followed the dwarfs to a large cavern dark and cold. They put their mounts into pens beside ponies already there. Children eyed them as they played.

Deeper and deeper into the mountain they went, along mazes of caverns. Jensen tried to keep track of where they went but lost it in the confusion of cross tunnels along the way. Recollection failed her as she strained to keep a return path in her mind. Jensen was the youngest and this was a task for her. If they had to escape they needed a route out of this mountain and she failed to provide one. She had failed herself and the others.

"Don't worry about finding a way back, Niki has set a spell illuminating an escape path that both of us can see," said Katie.

Sure tell me now thought Jensen.

Jensen was more than amazed by the sight before her as they left the tunnel and entered another cavern, but not just another cavern. It was an underground city as the cavern extended as far as the eye could see. There were streets with lampposts, signs, and walkways. Ponies pulled wagons making deliveries as dwarfs went about their daily business among children playing in the street.

At both sides of the cavern large holes in the mountain face let in light. Jensen could feel a strong breeze flowing around her as air moved from the cold lower tunnels into the cavern and out through the higher vents. The buildings were flat roofed made of rock and wood looking more like partitions than house. And the place was full of birds mostly barn swallows, sparrows and finches filling the air with sound. Jensen smiled at the sight and looked at Katie who was doing the same.

They walked along the street which looked to Jensen like a shopping centre for the town. There were large windows but the doors were of a height she would have to bend to enter. Inside the shops was a grand assortment of items the likes of which Jensen had never seen. The variety of goods was what amazed her, more than at the palace market by far. She had passed three jewellery stores already and by the looks of the people in the street their love for bobbles and beads was quite evident. Everyone had at least one necklace and more than one ring; brooches and pendants adorned all even the children. The artwork on jewellery looked the same where groups gathered or walked together making Jensen believe they were family or clan crests.

They finally ducked into a building full of soldiers and were escorted to a jail cell.

"In there," said the little man as he grinned from ear to ear.

"Raj Mituck," said Jensen as she'd had enough.

"No Jensen," said Niki grasping her arm, "Let me handle it."

They entered and sat on the tiny beds not long enough to lie on. They were made for lighter people and sagged. The cells had bars on three sides letting Jensen see that no others besides themselves were held in this place. Crime was not popular among the little folk it seemed or else execution was swift. The little man shut and locked the door; the very second he was clear Nikki raised her hand as though to shoo a fly. The door blew off its hinges slamming into the opposite wall. The steel was wedged into the rock several inches deep. The little man swallowed and lost his brazen look exchanging it for one of fear. Niki had had enough thought Jensen; so much for the little man and his condescending smile.

"Sorry, just a habit whenever somebody locks me in a cell," said Niki.

The little man quickly walked off.

"Why are we in here at all? Let's go," said Jensen.

Niki shook her head then said, "If we're going to roam around the mountain looking for a dragon, well, that's dangerous work. If we're going to fight all these dwarfs, that's also dangerous work. Doing both is double danger so let's see if we can't make peace with them. It won't hurt to make an alliance or friends if we can."

That made sense thought Jensen then wondered why she did not think of things like that. Maybe it was knowledge that comes with age.

After a while the little man returned with the key to the cell in his hands. He looked at it, shook his head and threw it to the wall near the embedded door. His look and demeanour had changed, a little tense but more humble in his way.

"My name is Tuck. I would consider it an honour if you would accompany me to dinner and then to see the king."

"We would be delighted and consider the honour as ours," said Niki with the grace of a Goddess.

A smile broke across Tuck's face and he nodded. Niki had a way of changing people thought Jensen; she had her own winning ways.

Not far from the prison was an inn but none like Jensen had ever seen. Besides too small chairs and tables it was spacious and catered more to meals than drink. Every ten or so little tables one was filled with plates of salads and condiments of all kind. They sat sideways at their table slightly hunched and waited for food to be served. It was as though he had prepared in advance as in minutes the meal was there. Jensen was amazed by the size of her serving; it was the one thing here that was not small. Even Tucks plate was huge and filled to overflowing; these little people ate like giants.

"You have an amazing city here, I'm sorry I've never heard of it or even knew of its existence, what is its name?" said Niki.

"We call it Taketslam, we're proud of it and our country Hur Nakim. We don't mix with others and see few strangers here."

"You shouldn't be shy, you have so much to offer and share with the world, so much to barter and trade. That's what I'd like to do, share our lands and talents with you," said Niki and Jensen saw the vixen in her.

"That would be up to king and not me, I'm the head of his army and nothing more," said Tuck.

"And a mighty army it seems, it looked as though there are a thousand or more," said Niki.

"Oh, three thousand and another three in reserve if needed," said Tuck proud as he sat stretching upward, sitting tall as he could.

Jensen listened to more as Niki stroked Tuck's ego. She was in command here, not him.

Next stop was the palace of the king and it would be the last if they made a mistake. Tuck explained that King Harden of Hur Nakim was as his name implied, a hard man of little patience and less humanity. They sat in silence as they waited for audience with him.

Tuck whispered in the king's ear and his eyes scanned them as he spoke. Jensen thought his words might not favour them and with her thumb stroked her ring. She glanced at Katie who looked ill at ease; Niki sat like stone and could not be read.

The king's face turned bitter; he had a scowl on the left side and a sneer on the right causing his upper lip to rise exposing his teeth. It seemed as if in deep hate he might burst forth and annihilate everything in sight.

"You come to conquer our land?" said King Harden.

Niki sat like a stone statue and did not answer him.

"Four witches come to us to poison our minds and turn clan against clan. Was that your idea?" added Harden.

Niki stood and slowly walked toward the king. She stopped a safe distance away, a look no one could read on her face. Jensen saw a look of awe on the faces of the dwarfs as they sat silent holding their breath.

"I am Nikita Princess of Tyhton," she said.

At those words sighs escaped then the mumbling began.

"Silence," yelled the king as he looked about then added, "you are the one who opposes Kamahl and stands in his way?"

"Yes I am," she said and more sighs filled the room and the mumbling resumed.

The king merely looked around him in anger and all lay in silence again.

"We have no love for Kamahl. He's ordered us to surrender our lands or he will take them at the cost of our lives. We will not surrender to him and will stand as you do."

"Let us stand together then and join forces on the day of the final battle. If that be your will," said Nikita.

"So it shall be whenever you give the word," said Harden another changed man.

Jensen thought that the woman had done it again. Women of fight and dreams could change the world.

"We have another purpose for being here. We come in search of the dragon Darrow. He has killed many in my land and I wish to speak to him to find the reason for him doing so," said Niki.

"You will be honoured guests while in our land but understand we have a pact with the dragons as well as you. I will however give you a guide for the sole purpose of finding him and discussing your differences," said the king.

"You are most generous kind sir. I look forward to our future endeavours and trade," said Niki.

"So be it then. I will turn you over to Olly our most knowledgeable guide and one of the oldest I might add. You'll find him invaluable for your task," said the king.

Jensen was impressed with the way Niki had handled the situation. Just enough force in her acts and ways as to not look weak. She was a true princess and diplomat who succeeded in uniting her people with the dwarfs.

They followed Tuck back to the cave entrance from whence they came. Jensen saddled biscuit and thought all was well. The old dwarf Olly came to them and was ready to lead. A day lost but new friends made they continued west in search of Darrow.

# THE GIFTED OF SISCERLY XXIII
## *Sophie the Dragon*

THEY MADE THEIR WAY west with Olly as a guide to help them find the cave where the dragon lived. Olly was one of the oldest dwarfs and knew every cave, cavern, and tunnel in the mountain range even the ones that had panned out and not been used in years or even centuries. Olly had learned the location of all the old mines by following his father as he made rounds searching for precious metals previously overlooked by others. Like his father before him Olly made a living the same way and had become a rich man as he found diamonds in a silver mine that had panned out.

They were riding towards an old coal mine abandoned for centuries. It would be a suitable place for a dragon's lair. According to their guide the mine had large entrances high on the mountain slopes where a dragon could fly from or land.

They reached a lush pasture where they hobbled their horses near the mine entrance. All except Biscuit were restrained as Jensen knew her little mare would never run away.

They followed Olly into the cave lighting lamps given

them by the dwarfs. They were lamps like Jensen had never seen, well crafted and glowing bright yet small. Olly led the way through the tall black tunnels. He explained that coal mines were larger than precious metal ones as little height or width was required to follow a gold vein whereas with coal the end product was a large chunk of the mountain itself. A dragon would live within a coal mine as far as Olly was concerned.

They were well on their way to the largest cavern of all a third of the way up the mountain. The path was steep at times causing Presela to have problems with the climb. Jensen held her left arm and steadied here as she went while Cromby tried to focus on the path ahead. It was a problem Presela always had as if her cat did not look straight ahead she would stumble over something unseen in the way. Curiosity was part of a cat's nature and Presela never cursed Cromby for being himself.

"Curiosity killed the cat, my mother used to say. Let's hope it doesn't get you both killed," said Jensen.

"Cromby is part of me; he's my eyes and the other half of my heart. He could never disappoint me in any way," said Presela.

That woman had a way of making Jensen feel small.

"Yah."

When they reached the huge cavern lamps were no longer needed as four large openings provided enough light to illuminate the cave. Only a few shaded areas behind rocks lay in darkness as Jensen boldly forged ahead. The others chose to look before they leapt but it was something the young enchantress never did. Like the cat Jensen was driven by curiosity and a blank mind.

"It's close, I can feel it," said Presela.

"Which way?" asked Jensen not stopping to look around.

The ground moved under Jensen's feet. A head larger than her body rose from the shadows and two big blue eyes stared into hers. Huge jaws opened exposing dagger teeth. A low roar with little sound shook the cavern. Jensen knew she had walked onto the sleeping beast and slowly moved to her right to get off. Jensen's gaze was locked on those big blue eyes occasionally slipping lower to look at wicked teeth.

Jensen felt solid rock under her feet and knew that she was clear. She looked downward and saw the dragon had made a bed within a recess filled with straw. Another roar louder than the first made her freeze as a huge jaw came close enough for her to touch. Then all was silent, the moment frozen in time. It seemed as though an eternity passed.

"Dragon. Are these your eggs?" yelled Niki. She was on the other side of the cavern thirty feet away.

"If you touch her I will destroy them," added Niki.

"No No she won't," yelled Presela as she moved closer and stood at Jensen's side.

"Niki get away from those eggs please, they're hers. She won't hurt us trust me please," said Presela.

The Dragon was lying down but slowly rose now standing on all four feet towering high over Jensen and Presela.

"It's not Darrow Niki. Her name is Sophie. She's Darrow's mate," said Presela.

Niki moved closer to Presela and Katie closed in as well. Jensen looked at both; Niki's hands were tightened into fists and she looked ready to explode. Katie held her snake belt in her right hand looking more than ready to fight.

"Don't ever threaten a dragon if you want to live," said Sophie in a low soft voice that sounded like a whisper but shook the stone beneath Jensen's feet.

"Why did your mate attack my castle and why on earth would he kill innocent people in the castle square?" asked Niki.

"The wizard Kamahl has put him under an ancient spell and through it forces him to do things he would not normally do. We have nothing to gain by raiding you. We do not need the same things you do and do not cherish gold. Darrow is a victim as much as you," said Sophie.

"What kind of a spell?" asked Jensen.

"I don't know. I wish I did. All I know is it didn't work on me," said Sophie.

"We'll get his true name and with it break the spell," said Niki.

Presela spoke immediately, "I think that would work. Everything on earth has a true name. With it the Gods can command one and make destiny come true."

"What's Darrow's true name Sophie?" asked Niki.

"I don't know? Neither does he. Who knows their true name anyway?"

"How do we find it?" asked Niki.

"We ask Kenji," said Katie.

"All right. It's all we can do so let's get started. I hope that Darrow doesn't kill anymore people for a while and I hope no one kills him," said Niki.

"It's going to take time. Four or five days one way," said Katie.

"Not if I take you," said Sophie.

"How?" asked Katie with a strange look on her face.

"On my back just above my shoulder. Like riding a horse," said Sophie.

Jensen's heart skipped a half dozen beats and she swallowed

at the thought of being lucky enough to ride a dragon. The others would all want to go as well so Niki would probably be the lucky one. She wouldn't stay silent though she would speak up.

"Wow, can I go?" asked Jensen, her eyes wide.

All looked at each other making strange faces and quiet then Katie laughed. The others joined in. They all looked relieved but how could that be? Jensen didn't care; she just wanted the honour of riding Sophie.

"Sure Jensen, we won't fight you for it," said Katie.

Niki shook her head and said, "How did I know she would want to do it? We'll wait for you at the dwarfs' cavern. Take care."

"You have no idea how much I didn't want to ride a dragon," whispered Katie to Niki and Presela.

"Oh yes I do. I wouldn't get on one of those if my life depended on it," whispered Presela.

Jensen petted Sophie and smiled proud to have a dragon as a friend.

"Why are you doing this Sophie?" asked Jensen.

"To help Darrow of course, I don't want him hurt."

Everyone except Jensen followed Olly out of the cave, all waving good bye to Jensen who was so filled with excitement she hardly noticed them at all. Jensen was glowing inside; she was going to ride a dragon, she was going to fly. Life couldn't possibly get any better than that. After this there was no place left to go, no adventure could ever top this thought Jensen. She wished the people from Cambells Cross could see her now. That thought brought on a hundred more dreams including the reason for being here. Jensen was here to save the lives of her parents and brothers.

"I can feel your sorrow from here," said Sophie.

"Kamahl has my parents and brothers. I have to get them free. I have to..," and Jensen started to cry.

Jensen had almost forgotten them; almost forgot while getting tangled in the excitement of her new life. How could she forget? They may even be dead while she flew around having fun.

"Let's do this first and after that we'll help you fight Kamahl?" said Sophie.

"Promise?"

"I promise and a dragon always keeps her word."

At one of the cave entrances high above the ground Jensen climbed up Sophie's right leg and onto her back. She sat in front of her shoulder and held onto a foot long spike, one of many running the length of her neck. Jensen was glad she wore thick leather pants as the scales were rougher than they looked. Without warning Sophie crouched low and at the same time spread her huge bat like wings. With a mighty push that pulled back at Jensen she rose onto her hind legs, and then with a downbeat of her wings took flight.

Jensen held tight to the spike with both hands and looked at the world below. Four tiny people were mounting horses and looking up at her. She waved as they did. They would all be sorry now they let her go, they would all be wishing they were up here instead.

Things appeared strange when seen directly from above; everything looked smaller: tiny trees, deer that looked like ants, and a giant lake they had passed by on the way was only the size of a wash bowl. Sophie flew higher and higher until she was in a cloud. The world below was lost for a time as Jensen felt clammy then wet.

"Hey Sophie, I'm soaked."

Sophie quit beating her wings and soared like an eagle dropping below the clouds. They drifted downward then a current of warm air brought them up to cloud level again. Sophie sought altitude to keep from being seen from below by Kamahl's troops. From the ground at this height she would look like a hawk. Jensen was amazed at the might of the wizard's force; the numbers were staggering, hard to believe. How would they ever defeat an army such as this?

To Jensen's right was the sea and the ruined temples she dreaded. They had covered two days travel on horseback in half a day. Sophie started to descend then dropped fast as an eagle diving for its prey. Jensen hung on tighter than ever as Sophie straightened and skimmed over the lake touching the water now and again. Slight sprays washed upward to cool Jensen who was already cold. The dragon beat her wings in a backward motion slowing to settle on the far shore.

"It's cold up there," said Jensen.

"I need water, so jump off. I'm going for a swim while I'm here," said Sophie.

Jensen walked along shore hugging herself to keep warm. She watched Sophie gulp water then dive low: she rolled left then right, flipped over backward, and put on quite a show. Jensen rubbed the inside of her numb thighs trying to get the blood to flow. Thank the Gods she wore thick leather riding pants or the inside of her thighs would be chafed. Those scales were rougher than they looked and were wearing after a time. But who was she to complain as they would make the whole journey in less than two days instead of five. All in all riding Sophie was not much harder than riding bareback on Biscuit and ten times as much fun. She would not tell Biscuit that though. Everyone should have a dragon Jensen thought; as long as they were as thoughtful as Sophie. Jensen was still cold so vigorously rubbed her arms and stomped her feet as she watched Sophie splash and play.

She never saw or heard the horse that knocked her to the ground.

Jensen lay with an ache in her left side and fought to breathe. Try as she might in her dazed state she could not draw a breath. Hands turned her and she lay on her back unable to fight. To the sound of laughter and the stench of unwashed men she fought for a breath. Jensen was too weak to use her power and could not utter the sounds to turn on the ring. She whispered the words with her last bit of air.

"Raj Mituck."

Now if Jensen could only think, only think of what she had to do next. Concentrate on those men, but could not. Jensen tried to breath. Hands grabbed the top of her shirt and she pushed them away. Big meaty hands then grabbed Jensen and lifted her off the ground then slammed her back into the dirt. Jensen gasped hard coughing and clearing whatever was in the way not allowing her to breathe. Without knowing the stranger had just saved her life. Jensen was about to thank him in her own special way by turning him against his friends. She would make them kill each other, so be it. Jensen could see now that six of Kamahl's thugs had come from the woods and gotten the best of her.

Then Jensen heard a bone chilling roar.

It was so loud it hurt her ears and made her curl up in a ball. Through the corner of her eye she saw the soldiers trying to keep control of their horses but soon failed. Their mounts ran away and the men turned drawing their swords to fight.

That was a mistake.

Sophie ran from the water and toward the armed men. At the last second the dragon turned with speed and grace. She flung her spiked tail at them knocking all the men down. Two lay unconscious and four struggled to their feet to be met head on by the dragon's front claws and teeth. A few groans and screams and it was over and done.

"Let's get out of here," said Sophie and Jensen agreed.

Jensen scrambled to get on the dragon's back as her left side screamed with pain. Soon they were over the Mensys River and headed toward the castle when Jensen pointed to a grove of trees. Sophie got the message and landed in a clearing beside a small stream.

"I don't think it wise to approach the castle right now. I know a farmer who lives just through those trees. You lay low and I'll get us something to eat," said Jensen.

"Agreed."

Jensen walked to the farmer's house her left side still in pain. She met Jed, her father's friend, at work in the barn as he did all day. She had always remembered him that way, a lifetime of toil in the barn tending hogs and cows.

"Uncle Jed, you're going to have to trust me today."

"Is that true what I hear about you liven at the palace now with the witches and things?" said Jed.

"Yes it's true, I'm fighting Kamahl and his soldiers trying to get mom and dad and my brothers back."

"Well whatever you need you got."

"Thanks Jed, load every scrap of food you can spare into that little wagon and help me drag it to the clearing by the stream. I can't do it myself; some soldiers almost killed me a couple of hours ago."

"What are you gonna feed an army or something."

"Yah, Something."

They loaded a wagon with a side of beef roast chicken and vegetables and more. Last on was a large keg of ale for Sophie and a bottle of wine for Jensen. Ethel, Jed's wife did nothing but complain but then she always did. Even if Ethel was having the time of her life all that came out of her mouth were complaints. Nothing was ever quiet right for her and nothing ever would be. Jed accepted that and so did everyone else, Ethel was Ethel and everyone let her be. Ethel complained about everything he took wanting to know why. She talked and talked while Jed as usual stayed silent then kissed her good bye.

Jed dragged the wagon to the clearing while Jensen walked at his side. Jed's eyes went wide when they arrived at the clearing.

"It's a dragon Jensen, run."

"It's Sophie and she's a friend, listen don't tell anyone you saw her."

"A dragon killed the Baker's boy at the market and some others too."

"It wasn't her. We're trying to stop the dragon that did it though, so relax she's as friendly as your pet goat."

"Good thing Ethel's not here."

"Yah, she would have something real to complain about though."

Sophie popped a side of beef in her mouth and in a minute it was gone. Jed took the wagon to get another and soon returned. This one was raw but Sophie didn't mind she ate all her meals that way. Jed said his good byes, even to Sophie and went his way. They would not see him for a while as at the crack of dawn they would be on their way. Jensen uncorked the keg of ale and set it in Sophie's mouth. Sophie tilted her head back and swallowed draining it as fast as it poured out. Jensen drank her wine and hoped it would kill the pain so she could sleep. Jensen curled up at Sophie's tummy as it was the warmest spot around. A wing came down and covered her making a nice warm nest.

"Don't roll over or I'll be a pancake."

"Don't worry I won't. Darrow says I sleep like a log."

Next morning at first light Sophie took flight as their journey continued to Kenji's mountain. Half a day later they arrived at Kettle Peak. Jensen pointed to the horse trail leading to the unseen opening in the cave. Sophie landed and Jensen jumped down. With the wave of her hand the cave entrance appeared and both went inside. A transparent image of Kenji appeared.

"I thought I'd better greet you here as I don't think you will both fit through the tunnels," said Kenji.

"This is Sophie and I hope she's welcome here. We are in dire need of you and had no time for me to come forward alone and ask," said Jensen.

"If you travel here with good will in your heart then you're welcome," said Kenji.

"We seek the true name of her mate Darrow. Kamahl has put him under a spell and is using the spell to make Darrow do his bidding. How do I find his true name?" said Jensen.

"Go to the Isle of the Gods and seek out the priestess Ises. Ises will know how to get it but whether she does is anybody's guess. Ises hates Kamahl with a passion you could never know but is so unpredictable in all she does. Don't trust her as she serves only herself. Be very careful on this you two but she's the only one who can help," said Kenji.

They said a quick good bye and followed Kenji's instructions on how to find the Isle of the Gods.

# THE GIFTED OF SISCERLY XXIV
## *The Serpent Soldiers Arrive*

KATIE LIKED WATCHING NIKI work and that's exactly what she did every minute of the day. She was the Princess of Tyhton and had a country to lead. She seized that role with the ferocity of a tiger, fought and laboured relentlessly for the land she loved. She was trying to convince King Harden to build a seaport so that shipping could commence between their countries.

"I will at my expense send ships north with farm goods which I see you're always short of," explained Niki, "We will trade for your metal work, weapons, lamps, and such, things of which you have in abundance."

"We're not used to dealing with the outside world and a port would also be an invasion point for a tyrant like Kamahl," said King Harden.

"Kamahl's invasion will come from land, not from the sea. His magic rides on the backs an enormous army. A port would serve to bring help to you should you need it," said Niki.

"Well we'll see. I'll meet with the council of elders and

we'll discuss the matter. For now it's time and we will feast," said Harden.

Katie knew that when the dwarfs' dinner bell rang they answered it immediately and would think of nothing else. They left the king's court where he conducted the business of his tiny country and crossed the square to the dinning hall. They all sat at tiny tables and again Katie struggled to sit almost kneeling on the tiny chair. Katie smiled at Niki who was a shade taller than her doing the same. Presela did not likebeing short but at times like this it was an asset.

That night was the same as the one before as the dwarfs were slaves to their daily procedures and customs. They ate at precisely the same time, retired at ten strokes of their big clock and rose every morning when daylight pierced through the cavern openings in their mountain dome.

The next morning would not be the same.

"Kamahl's forces are here," said Presela with a gasp.

Niki ran to tell the king who quickly sent out scouts.

Bugles and gongs sounded throughout the dome as dwarfs feverishly raced to assigned posts. Katie, Niki and Presela raced to the king's court where Tuck sat wiping sweat from his brow; the look of horror and fear on his face.

"How many?" asked Niki.

"About ten thousand, almost twice our force," said Tuck.

"That's why Kamahl's reinforcements were so slow in coming to Tyhton. He wants to take the land of the Dwarfs first. Doesn't want them at his back," said Katie.

"Now that we've stopped him cold he has to look at other options and yes the dwarfs at his back are a threat," agreed Niki.

The court was in turmoil, all argued and it seemed no one could agree.

"We'll attack them before they even get to the mountains or our homes," yelled King Harden.

All were silent as Tuck, commander of the army rose to his feet.

"I don't think you want to do that, I'm sorry for interrupting but I think it's a bad idea," said Niki causing Tuck to stop dead in his tracks.

"I won't have fighting around women and children in the cities and towns," said the king.

"If you meet his army in the open you will be outnumbered and fighting a war on his terms. Kamahl has spell casters, catapults, and other weapons of war. In my country I sacrificed the northern half and stood at the Mensys River which the wizard has yet to cross. If you meet him in the open he will destroy you in a day. You must make him split his forces and come after you.

"Trick his commanders into the mountains so that your tunnels are in front of them and behind. Attack in small forces then run and fight him in caves that you know. Force them to break up and chase you, fight on your terms not his.

"You have an advantage in that they don't know that Katie, Presela, and I are here. We will know what their plans are thanks to Presela and Katie and I will set traps."

"You will help us?" asked the king.

"Of course, we are allies, we stand at your side," said Niki.

"You and Tuck will engage them then," ordered the king.

Tuck smiled and ran to Niki like a child to a mother's side. They left court and made for the stables to retrieve their horses.

"Presela try to read what you can from them but take care not to alert their spell casters, we can't let them know we're here," said Niki.

"Tuck, send a commander with about five hundred men a long way west so that it looks as though the force they seek is waiting for them there and not here."

"Come on Katie, let's have a look," said Niki.

Katie knew that Niki would take command; she was the commanding type. Wherever Niki was she towered above all. People expected her to take control; just like Tuck a minute ago. Tuck was waiting for orders and really it was his army and not hers but that's how people were around the princess.

They rode east and then slightly south and there they were, big and bold, in the distance moving their way. Katie could just barely make out the wooden covered wagons like the ones gypsies used. Their spell casters, and there were a lot as she counted four wagons in a row. Kamahl must have expected trouble with the dwarf's tunnels.

"I wished Jensen was here," said Katie.

"She should be back in three days or so, I hope. You're right we could certainly use her. Strange thing isn't it Katie. Only a month ago it looked like we wouldn't stand a chance and now with the help of that little lady we can defeat and even hope to destroy Kamahl. Never give up hope," said Niki.

"If we force them to fight in the caves it will render their catapults useless and also limit what their spell casters can do. You're definitely right, we have to get them to chase us no matter what it takes," said Katie.

"We'll put the women and children in one place under that big domed city they call Taketslam. I can set up wards and webs as traps to protect them while we fight. We don't have the men to guard them," said Niki.

With that in mind they returned to Taketslam and explained their plans to the king. The dwarfs rounded up peasants from mining towns and villages, some almost a day away.

"It'll take Kamahl's troops the rest of the day to get here and another to set up camp and their defences. We'll have lots of time to ready for them. I'll protect Taketslam with magical webs. None of their spell casters will get through what I construct as long as we don't give them the time. So keep an eye out for them day and night then kill them or chase them away but don't give them time to figure out what I've put down," said Niki to the king and his war council.

Katie watched them argue amongst themselves as though unable to decide, even when no decision was to be made. Niki was an ambassador as well as a princess so had the patience to wait for someone to confirm what she had already decided to do. Katie knew she would never have the tolerance that Niki had. It's not that Katie was rude just quiet; she would say nothing and walk away from the fools and do whatever she was going to do.

"Ah, yes well then go ahead, we support your decision," said King Harden.

"I'll take leave and return when finished," said Niki.

The next day from a mountain cave Katie, Niki, Presela, and Tuck watched as Kamahl's commanders set up camp.

"Who's in command Presela?" asked Niki.

"The tall muscular one drinking from a bottle by the big yellow tent. His name is Carp and he's the best they've got. Half of what Kamahl has sent are seasoned troops."

"What's his plan?" asked Niki.

"To draw us out in the open of course, the opposite of our intentions."

"How does he plan to do that?" asked Niki.

"Wait. He thinks you're going to come out and drive him away," said Presela.

"He'll have a long wait," said Niki.


Katie knew that all of Kamahl's commanders worked on one basic principle and that was greater numbers than their opponents. Even the brilliant ones if he had any were not as bright as a captain in Niki's army. So Carp would try this and that and if he ran short of men would simply send for more. Sooner or later he would succeed and overthrow the dwarfs. Throwing numbers of soldiers at his enemies was his only plan against which there was no defence. Through Kamahl Carp had almost an endless supply of fighting men from his own lands and others he had taken so far. Countless numbers of mother's sons would die here in the next few days.

Katie wished Jensen was here. That little girl turning into a woman had more heart than anyone Katie had ever known. Katie knew that most of the time she was a frightened little girl playing tough and living off raw nerves. Jensen did like Sophie though and the idea of flight did not scare her in the least. If Jensen had not volunteered no one else would have either, that much Katie knew. They were all relieved and would never trade places with her, not in a million years. Katie smiled whenever she thought of Jensen and wished she'd had a daughter like her.

# THE GIFTED OF SISCERLY XXV
## *The Trouble with Ises*

THE ANGRY SEA LASHED up at them for daring to fly over its turbulent path. Below Jensen and Sophie the waves reached skyward wanting to pull them in to its watery depth. It wasn't only the rain, although that was bad enough, but the head wind was almost as fast as Sophie could fly. And far worse than everything else were the lightning bolts that seemed to barely scrape by. Sophie tried to get above the weather but it was not possible as the farther up she went the colder it turned. Jensen would not be able to bare the frigid temperatures above the churning clouds. Sophie would not turn back and wait. She worried about Darrow, her mate. So here they were, Sophie straining against the wind with a long way to go before reaching a shore.

Jensen lay flat on Sophie's back hanging onto a spike with both hands. It seemed an eternity had passed since they had started their trek into this gloom. They had barely advanced at all and were fighting to inch their way to a destination of many miles or more. Jensen was wetter than wet, soaked as water overflowed from her boots. Her clothes were stuck tight to her body and she was also more than merely cold; she was almost frozen stiff and could barely move.

It was so hot and humid on the ground that the thought of cold never entered her mind. She cursed herself for not wearing a coat but then how could she know what flying was really like. Sophie pushed on without missing a beat but could and should have gone back. With the winds behind them they could soar home and wait another day but the dragon would not. Dragons were stubborn Jensen concluded, as obstinate as she.

At the very second Jensen thought she was loosing her grip and might fall lightning flashed exposing an island ahead. With a grunt and renewed hope Jensen clamped her frozen hands tight as she could around the spike and held on.

Sophie landed on a beach and walked to a grove of trees not far from shore. The overhead canopy of leaves was a dry shelter from the storm. The tired dragon collapsed after Jensen jumped to the ground. She petted Sophie's nose and gave her a kiss then crawled under an extended wing for warmth. Both were too tired to speak and sleep found them quickly that night.

Jensen woke that morning hungry and still wet. Hunger was the first thing to be resolved so she sloshed around in her wet boots searching for food. Nuts and berries would do for starters then she realized it was too early in the season for both. The berries would be green and the nuts still high in the trees. She returned and woke Sophie who was still tight asleep.

"Let's fly up and take a look around," said Jensen.

Sophie stretched and yawned then slowly rose. Without warning she vigorously shook herself like a dog. Water flew in huge drops wetting Jensen's clothes again after they'd started to dry.

"Hey thanks."

"Quit complaining, jump up and let's go. The air will dry you."

High above the island they found the buildings including the temple they were searching for. The only problem was Kamahl's soldiers were all over the grounds. Sophie had been flying high enough not to be noticed and only dove to identify whose soldiers they were. That snake emblem on the tents and flags belonged to Kamahl. The dragon picked a clearing not far from the temple and landed.

"You stay here Sophie; I'll go take a look."

"Careful now, you remember what happened the last time you played with soldiers by the lake."

"Hey, those caught me off guard."

"Make sure these don't."

"All right, I'll be back soon."

Jensen snuck through the bush, her boots still making squishing sounds. Jensen sat and removed them then carefully walked barefoot on the rough forest ground. Step by step with caution in mind she edged her way to the temple and the soldier's tents. Sophie was not going to let her forget her mistakes so she had better not make any today. She wanted no surprises in any case and was here looking for a dragon's true name not a fight.

Jensen spotted the soldiers to her left and skirted farther right. Through a clearing of waist high grass she half crept eyeing the soldiers on the way. Jensen would make no mistakes; take all the time needed and stay low.

Jensen tripped over two pairs of legs lying in the grass.

A soldier and a young woman gasped in surprise as she fell beside both. Before the soldier could reach for a weapon or call in alarm she had a hand on his wrist.

"Stand down soldier and be quiet," said Jensen.

Jensen's magic cut off the soldier's shout and only a soft note escaped. The young woman looked on in fear. The young woman was bigger than her and Jensen hoped the woman would not fight. How could the woman know the witchcraft she had just seen worked only on men?

"Don't shout. I'm no threat to you. I only wish to speak to Ises," said Jensen.

The young woman looked at her still in fear and did not speak. She raised her hand and shook the soldier as he sat in his calm, paralysed state.

"How did you do that?" she finally said.

"A little trick I know, what's your name?"

"Sandra. Is he going to be all right?"

"Yes, in a day or so. Will you take me to Ises?"

The woman stood straight but Jensen still crouched low.

"It's all right you can stand and walk normally. They'll think you're one of the slaves," said Sandra.

They both walked toward the temple and soon arrived; the soldiers far to the left did not even look their way.

Sandra held Jensen's arm and pleaded, "Don't tell Ises about the soldier please. I'm a priestess in training and we're not allowed with men."

"It's our secret."

Once inside Sandra talked to a woman about Katie's age. The woman immediately walked Jensen's way.

"Well, well, what do we have here?" said the woman.

"My name is Jensen and if you're Ises then I need your help."

"I'm Ises. Do you always carry your boots?"

"Oh, they're wet from the storm last night," said Jensen as she set them on the floor.

"How did you get here?"

Jensen thought for a moment as Kenji's words ran through her mind. Kenji called her devious and told her not to trust Ises but the subject of dragons and their names was going to come up. How much would she tell her? Then Jensen realized she needed her help and would sooner or later have to tell all.

"On Sophie, she's a dragon, I flew."

Ises eyes went wide then she smiled and finally laughed.

"You had me for a minute there. What else, a silly question on my part, you came by boat."

"No, dragon. She's in a clearing not far, want to see her?" said Jensen and without waiting for an answer continued, "We have a problem. Kenji sent us. Sophie, the dragon, well it's about her mate Darrow. He's under a spell cast by Kamahl and does his bidding. We need to know his true name so we can free him from the wizard. That would work wouldn't it?" said Jensen.

"Knowing his real name would give you total power over him, so yes he would be at your command and could not listen to Kamahl."

"Could you give us his true name then please?" asked Jensen.

Ises stood and pondered at Jensen's request and Kenji's words again rang through Jensen's mind. It was a simple question but the woman was probably going through options and would do whatever served her best.

"Giving you a true name is not as simple as it sounds. You have to give me some information about the dragon. Then I have to ask the Gods and if they deem it a reasonable request will grant it and tell me the name. If they do not judge it worthy they may not even answer me. Either way the wait could be long."

"Please try, I have no other choice," said Jensen.

"All right, point out on the wall map behind you where he lives and give me the name his mate calls him."

Jensen sat and waited as Ises knelt before an altar. Jensen's stomach was too empty to make a sound. Hours passed and Jensen thought of nothing but food feeling a though she would faint. Jensen's waist was drawn in and so tight that she had to keep pulling her pants up lest they fall. At the far end of the room Jensen watched women take food from the kitchen to yard. Finally Ises returned with a blank look on her face.

"Nothing yet," she said.

"Do you have an apple or something?" asked Jensen.

"Oh yes, we'll get you something."

Ises started to walk away when the temple door opened and six soldiers entered, two supporting the man Jensen had put in a trance earlier that day.

"Who are you?" demanded the commander.

"Jensen, I'm here to pray."

"How did you get here?"

"By boat."

"There's no boat in the harbour. Come with us you've got questions to answer."

"Raj Mituck."

Jensen looked into the commanders eyes then took his hand. Jensen knew the most power came from her gift when she had contact with the man. Jensen glanced at the other soldiers to calm them; it was the way her gift worked.

"Commander stand down, relax. You will not report to Kamahl after this day but instead will be led by Ises from now on as will the rest of your soldiers. Come with me and we'll tell the others," said Jensen.

Jensen held the commander's hand and left the temple for the soldier's camp. They smiled seeing him with a new love but their faces took on a serious look after staring into Jensen's eyes. She told them that they now served Ises and their enemy was Kamahl.

The second she finished and started to turn was when her world went dark.

# The Gifted of Siscerly XXVI
## *Sophie takes Charge*

Jensen had a headache second to none; it hurt all the way to her toes. Her teeth ached, she could barely see from her right eye but her hunger was there no more. What made her think of hunger at a time like this? Oh yes, she was going to eat when all this started. All what? Jensen felt a bandage around her head soaked in blood. At least somebody cared whether she lived or died. Someone had the decency to wrap her bleeding head after they had tried to split it open. Who said people weren't kind anymore?

Jensen surveyed the room: a bed, a table, a closet, and some chairs. She tested the door but it was locked. She would climb out the window, had done that before but couldn't find a window. There wasn't one. Jensen sat on the edge of the bed and thought then remembered it all.

How stupid could she be?

Jensen had turned over command of Kamahl's soldiers to Ises. The woman Kenji warned her not to trust. Jensen had freed the priestess as a favour for giving her the true name of

Darrow. But come to think of it she'd not given her a name. Jensen had thought it odd that Ises had spent so much time at the alter talking to her Gods yet came back empty handed or maybe not.

Jensen's wondered what the woman had to gain. What could making her a prisoner possibly accomplish? Sell her to Kamahl?

Suddenly the door opened and Ises walked in accompanied by two of her priestesses.

"Well, how do you feel young lady?" asked Ises.

"Why did you hit me?" asked Jensen.

"Clever aren't we. You knew it was me."

"Not clever at all, I'm a prisoner. Why?"

"You're an enchantress my dear and I as a high priestess know what an enchantress can do. You have more power than others in tales I've heard or read about. You're the greatest asset I could come upon.

"You'll build me an army second to none and I'll rule the richest land in the world. You'll be able to walk into the treasure cellars of all the great kings and get them to help you carry the booty out."

"It doesn't work like that. If I go up against a hundred men, I'm dead. I only have the strength for a few at a time, like the commander and his men. This one was easy because I had the commander in my hand and his men did not oppose me at all. Had they been ready and waiting for me an arrow would probably have killed me. It's easy for my magic to work on unsuspecting men," said Jensen.

"So we'll build the empire slowly but build it we shall. Without you I'm nothing, no one will follow me after loosing five thousand men to Kamahl. He made me the laughing stock of the world and I will destroy him with your help.

"You want him dead and out of the way as much as I. We'll free your parents and brothers, oh yes, I know. Remember I'm a Seer, probably the greatest in the world. Believe me, you're with me like it or not, so you may as well accept fate and me," said Ises.

"You can't hold me prisoner. Sophie will come for me and if not her then somebody else," said Jensen.

"I've already seen Sophie and told her to fly away or I'd kill you and fly she did."

"Would you kill me, I mean really kill me just for not following you?" asked Jensen. She had to know.

"I'll see you dead before I give you up."

Jensen believed her and knew that she was fighting for her life but would not stay. One way or another she would have to get out. Ises was a tyrant same as Kamahl. All tyrants were fickle from one day to the next depending on what they wanted. Jensen in her short life had learned that much so far. And Kenji was right; Jensen should never have turned her back on the priestess.

As for Sophie; what was it Sophie said to Niki as she stood over her eggs? "Never threaten a dragon if you want to live." She couldn't see Sophie flying away running from a threat. What was the dragon up to?

"Let's go we are going to give you a bath then feed you something. You'll have two female attendants with you at all times when you leave your room, and oh yes, me," said Ises.

They went to a bathhouse not far from the temple; the soldiers were far away. Jensen smiled knowing Ises would not let her near any men as she would soon enlist them in her fight to be free. Jensen objected to being washed; she'd bathed on her own since her fourth birthday. She didn't like being pawed at by giggling women. They dressed her in a white robe like theirs; oh great, she was one of them.

It was a clear sunny day when they left the bath house so Jensen thought it odd when a large shadow like that of a cloud fell upon them.

Two great claws surrounded Ises and scooped her up.

Jensen ducked to avoid being slapped by one of Sophie's great wings. Ises dangled under Sophie as she was carried over the trees and out of sight. The soldiers stood bows in hand but did not fire probably afraid to hit their Queen. Jensen returned to the bath house and put on her leather travelling garb. Jensen knew those clothes would be needed soon. Never threaten a dragon if you want to live; she'd have to remember that.

Jensen sat on the temple steps head in hands. Her attendants were lost without Ises. They didn't have a clue what to do now that she was gone. They looked to the sky and prayed for her return. If the priestess died then sooner or later they would starve.

Half a day passed when Sophie returned with Ises dangling from her front claws. The dragon set Ises down before the temple; the priestess collapsed. Ises was still conscious but definitely shaken.

"If you were the greatest Seer in the world then why didn't you see that coming?" said Jensen.

Ouch, that must have hurt.

The soldiers were still in the background not loosing arrows still afraid to hit Ises, their queen.

"So they caught you off guard again," said Sophie

Jensen could swear there was a smile on the dragon's face.

Jensen knew that Sophie would never let her live this one down but was not going to dignify her comment with an answer so let it lie.

"You got Darrow's true name didn't you?" said Jensen.

"Ironclaw."

Jensen knew that she had extracted that little bit of information from Ises. That's why Sophie snatched Ises and not her. If Sophie had grabbed her instead of the priestess it would have been a wasted trip. Ises was a mortal and could be made to talk. Anybody could dangle from a dragon's claws high above the clouds.

"How high did you take her before she spilled the name?" asked Jensen.

"Up to where you people freeze."

And it would be the right name as the priestess would not want to spend the rest of her life in a hole. If Ises crossed Sophie then the priestess would know that she could be scooped up again; any time, anywhere.

"Let's get out of this place," said Jensen.

Ises stood as they flew off and strangely enough waved. She also held her arm in the air toward her soldiers telling them to back off. They did not fire a single arrow at Sophie. Ises knew that a battle with a dragon would not end well for any of them. Ises was a tyrant but no fool. The priestess could loose with grace but fought to win. That's the problem with tyrants, they were always under control.

The sky was a bright blue and only a few puffy clouds hung in the air. There was a cool breeze at their back aiding their flight and they soon found the coast. Jensen still had not eaten and neither had Sophie so like it or not they would have to stop at Jed's farm again.

"I'm sorry Jed but I had no where else to go. I haven't eaten in over two days and neither has Sophie. As soon as I get back to Siscerly I'll get Amie to send someone out with payment, honest," said Jensen.

"It's all right. I don't mind helping out with the war and all, it's all right."

"I also need a warm coat, a hat, and a pair of mittens," said Jensen.

"It's a hot summer day Jensen. Why would you need that?"

"It's freezing up there believe it or not. I don't know why but the closer I get to the sun the colder it gets," said Jensen.

In the grove of elm trees by the stream they chewed on another meal compliments of Jed.

"Where is Kamahl keeping Darrow?"

"Darrow said he was told to wait at Stone Ridge, a castle not far from Kamahl's court," said Sophie.

"Think we should check it out?" said Jensen.

"We could go and take a look. It wouldn't hurt."

Jensen put on her wool coat, hat, and mittens then mounted Sophie. The dragon would have to fly high to avoid being seen not only by ground troops but also by Kamahl's magic. Katie had told her that the wizard surrounded his castles with wards and webs of all sorts. It would be hard to get in or out without his knowing especially after having lost his seer, Presela. The wizard would be on his guard.

They flew all day and finally found the castle at Stone Ridge. It was still daylight so they landed in the woods not far away and waited for dark.

The moon was a little more than half full peeking through transparent clouds. There was sufficient light to drop into the castle and look around. And that's what Sophie did; literally dropped in, landing in the middle of the main court yard. Not a complicated plan.

Darrow was lying against the east wall, asleep.

Jensen jumped from Sophie's back and ran toward the guards at the main gate to stop them from sounding the alarm.

She failed.

Soldiers poured out of the barracks.

"Raj Mituck."

Jensen ducked swords while Sophie fought. It was not the type of fight Jensen wanted any part of so she made her way toward Darrow. It was too dark for her to make eye contact with the soldiers and armed with shields and swords it would be hard to get a hold of them.

Darrow woke and snapped at Jensen almost taking off her right arm.

"Stand down Ironclaw. You are no longer under Kamahl's spell and will listen only to me or Sophie."

Darrow's big eyes went wide as he pondered over her words. Jensen caught a glimpse of a soldier behind her raising his sword. So did Darrow and he snapped up the man and tossed him across the wall.

"Glad to have you on our side," said Jensen.

Out of a castle door came a tall man dressed completely in black. His face was unreadable, his manner calm. He raised his hand and a bolt of lightning shot toward Sophie hitting her in the left side. She lunged in pain and roared.

It was Kamahl.

What was he doing here?

Darrow ran to his mate's aid and caught a lightning bolt

that sent him tumbling to the ground. The wizard showed no concern battling two dragons at one time.

"Kamahl you piece of crap, try me on for size," said Jensen.

The wizard seemed to shrink as he turned to avoid her direct stare. Kamahl sent one of his lightning bolts at Jensen but it had no affect at all. It only filled her with energy. Jensen knew her strength had grown since their last meeting and so did he.

She saw fear in the wizard's eyes.

"Angel get out here," yelled Kamahl.

From the same door that Kamahl came from a female warrior appeared. Dressed in black leather, armed with a sword and a battle axe, she came Jensen's way.

Jensen was so close.

Just one touch and Kamahl would turn to dust and cease to exist. It could all be over in seconds if she could get past that iron maiden dressed in black. But Jensen had almost been killed by a woman like her a few weeks ago.

"Let's get out of here," yelled Jensen.

Jensen ran toward Sophie passing close to Kamahl. He darted into a castle out of harms way.

So close.

The female warrior was closing in as Jensen ran up Sophie's leg and sat on her shoulders. The warrior followed but was caught off guard when Jensen planted both of her feet directly into the woman's face. The woman of the Koto-Ri tumbled to the ground. The dragons took flight stirring the grounds below as the beating of their wings sent debris into the air.

Jensen surveyed the damage on Sophie and Darrow while

in mid flight. Both were bleeding from wounds caused by the lightning bursts.

"Can you make it back to Jed's farm?" yelled Jensen.

"I'll try," said Sophie.

Jensen eyed Darrow also bleeding from his chest and left side. They flew high keeping out of arrow range.

At the grove of elms on Jed's farm the dragons drank from the stream.

"I'll ride to Siscerly to get Amie. She can heal your wounds," said Jensen.

At the palace Jensen searched for Amie and finally found her at the market giving stone mason's instructions for some work that needed to be done.

"You want me to what?" said Amie.

"Heal two dragons and I know one of them Darrow burned the market but it was not his fault. Kamahl had a spell on him. But he's all right now. Please Amie," said Jensen.

"I'll do it for you but certainly not for them. I trust you know what you're doing."

"They're friends now, thanks Amie. You won't regret it, you'll see. Oh and I'll need two wagon loads of beef. One for Jed and one for Sophie and Darrow," said Jensen.

"What, we're going to feed them for burning down the market now, reward them for killing people, that's going to far," said Amie, quite angry.

"Trust me Amie, please," said Jensen but got no response.

They arrived at the clearing Sophie and Darrow still bleeding. Two wagons full of beef followed them, one for Jed and the other went to the clearing.

"I've never healed a dragon before but it should be the same as a horse," said Amie looking over Sophie.

Amie ran her hands over the wounds on the dragon's side. As she did the skin and scale grew over the wound with a pinkish tint where before there was torn flesh.

"That feels better much better now. Thank you very much Amie," said Sophie.

Amie was concentrating and did not answer. The sorceress went to Darrow and looked at his wounds halting in thought. Darrow saw the look on her face.

"It's all right if you do nothing. I know you do not want to heal me. I'm sorry for what I've done. I'll try to make it up to you somehow," said Darrow.

"Well you can't make it up if you're bleeding to death. Remember dragon you owe me one," said Amie.

Darrow did not answer as Amie patched his wounds the same as the sorceress had done for Sophie. Only pink scales remained, the bleeding had stopped.

"Rest for at least today. I've cast a spell to kill the pain but it will return in about two days. It shouldn't be too bad though," said Amie.

Amie turned to walk away then stopped in thought the said, "Don't forget dragons. You owe me one."

"Thanks Amie, you're the best big sister a girl could ever have," said Jensen.

Jensen gave Amie a hug before the sorceress left. They unhitched the panicky horses from the wagon. The wagon shook as the dragons unloaded it with their great jaws. To Darrow half the wagon full of beef was probably just a snack.

The next morning Jensen climbed on Sophie's shoulder and they flew north with Darrow at her side, the way it should be.

# The Gifted of Siscerly XXVII
## *The Serpent Soldiers Attack*

Neither Tuck nor Olly could give Niki a count on the number of tunnels in the mountain range. Both claimed they numbered hundreds, some natural, and some man made. The tunnels leading to Taketslam, the domed city, were complex with many bends and intersections before arriving. The chances of Carp's serpent soldiers finding them were slim. If it were found and attacked in mass then it could be evacuated. A long tunnel ran under the mountains to the coast.

If Carp's serpents entered the tunnels in force they would be fighting a war they couldn't possibly win; they didn't know the lay of that battlefield. The dwarfs did.

Niki knew the only thing Carp could do was to siege the mountain stronghold in hopes of starving the dwarfs and forcing them out. With access to the coast that was highly unlikely. Did Carp not know the extent of the tunnels? Was Niki missing something?

Niki wondered about it then came to the conclusion that Carp underestimated the dwarfs. Carp probably thought that because of their short stature their other attributes were equally lacking. He'd made a mistake, a tactical error. One on one the dwarfs were as tough as his brawniest soldiers and just as strong with courage to match.

Over the next two days the enemy camp stretched west along the mountain range. It was well done as no groups were isolated; no weakness that could be taken advantage of. So they were under siege, simple as that.

King Harden sat in contemplation as the council of elders argued over what was to be done. Finally he stood stone faced and stared around the room; complete silence filled the air.

"I will not have these invaders on my land. I will not cease to live or fulfill my destiny because they tell me to. I will not let these people stand at my front door and threaten my life. I will not live day to day fearing they will come inside.

"We have worked for centuries to build what we have. Now men come and claim it for themselves. They tell us to give it to them or take it they shall.

"I for one would rather destroy what we have built than give it to these men. They tell us to voluntarily become their slaves or they shall slaughter us. Before I would enslave myself to them I would rather die; die in battle not at the end of a whip.

"How dare they think they can walk into my land and make those demands. In what they do they look down on me as though I was a lesser man. They insult me and my people in what they have already done and what they threaten to do.

"I personally can do nothing less than put on my armour and with my war axe fight these men. Who will follow?"

The room broke into a single deafening roar loud as any beast in the land.

Niki had renewed respect for King Harden after hearing his speech. She felt he was true to his words. The spirit he showed was not only his but that of his people as well.

Niki, Katie, Tuck, and Olly stood on a high mountain entrance to the dragon's lair and looked to the soldiers below. The line of troops ended at this point. According to Olly the caves through an obscure route ran farther west so there were entrances beyond the soldiers. Another tactical error by Carp; his scouts had missed some caves to the west.

That night two thousand dwarf soldiers wearing armour padded with cloth and weapons in hand moved silently through the night. Everything that clicked or clanked had been muffled before they reached the soldiers. Their plan was simple; attack the tail of the snake taking as many lives as possible then race back into the caves and get lost. Niki and Katie led the way checking for magical wards and webs.

Niki's lightning bolts lit up the night as a dozen serpent soldiers fell. The attack was swift as Niki, Katie, and the dwarfs moved east following the line of troops. Dwarf archers high above in entrances to the dragon's lair and other high cave openings rained arrows on the serpents below. They were guided by the dim light of the camp fires and the noise of the soldiers and the clattering of their armour.

The archers succeeded in breaking up the line formation leaving about three thousand serpent troops cut off from the rest. The element of surprise caused chaos among the serpent soldiers. Its value was never as obvious to Niki as it was this night. Who would have expected an attack at all?

Niki and Katie ignited tents and wagons using their power whenever they could. Katie's skill with a broad sword was second to none. Niki pushed with both hands at soldiers rushing her way. With chants and her power she sent masses of compressed air rushing toward them. They hit like rocks on glass. It was as though twenty men were smashed by invisible charging wild boars, their broken bodies were flung aside.

Three thousand serpent soldiers lay dead long before the arrival of dawn. The dwarfs carried their own wounded back to the cave entrances hotly pursued by serpent troops from the east. The serpent soldiers did not follow into the caves fearing a trap.

At dawn Niki heard a captain report the body count to Tuck. Five hundred dwarfs killed last night and about three thousand of the enemy. Niki would have been saddened if only one dwarf had died but the number she heard brought tears to her eyes that she hid from the others.

The next day Niki watched from above as the line of tents, wagons, and horses were drawn into a single camp of about seven thousand soldiers well out of arrow range from the mountains. Mounted scouting parties moved east and west.

In retaliation Carp sent death squads of up to a thousand men on raids into the tunnels. Vengeance must have burned deep for him to make such a mistake. Niki and Tuck would take advantage of his errant ways.

In one case a squad of five hundred men turned into a dead end mine shaft. A dwarf captain had seen them go in so knocked down the supporting beams at the entrance sealing them in for all time. The dwarfs set traps collapsing both ends of a tunnel after serpent soldiers entered.

Niki and Katie did their share killing hundreds in days with magic. The fifth day after his terror campaign turned against him Carp sent no soldiers into the tunnels. Niki estimated both side to be even now at about for thousand men each.

King Harden hearing the news gave explicit orders. Fearing reinforcements were coming to Carp the dwarfs were to attack and kill every last serpent soldier.

Niki in no way liked Harden's plan as the loss of life would be high on their side leaving few soldiers alive in the end to defend the realm of the dwarfs. But if reinforcements came for Carp it would put them in the same position that they were in from the start, outnumbered and under siege. Niki had to admit there was no other option. If they won they would send a signal to Kamahl; he would have to send a major force or none at all. He would have to pull troops from other lands leaving him weak in those spots.

The next day fighting was brutal neither side giving way. Men died but no ground was gained by either one. As Niki fought she could only think of the waste of lives, all due to the greed of one man and the cowardly wizard wasn't even near the battlefield.

Niki fought with all her might against their spell casters disabling almost all. Her energy was almost gone as her rings glowed dim, drained. The sorceress was of little use with weapons as Katie was. The witch had no equal with that golden blade, fending off two serpents at a time.

Niki had only the energy in her body left so could fight only in defence of her life. Then she saw a shadow cast over the battle ground and felt a fluctuating wind.

"YAH HOOO, Raj Mituck."

Niki looked high at the sound as two dragons descended into the fight. Both landed shooting flames from their mouths. Jensen jumped form Sophie's back entering into the battle as well. Jensen used her power over men turning enemy soldiers against each other. On either side of her the dragons fought with flames, claws, and dagger teeth. The last of Carp's soldiers including Carp himself fled from the fight. They didn't stop at their camp, just fled the country while they still could.

"We thought you'd deserted us," said Katie.

"No, I got caught up fighting Kamahl. Oh Katie it was so close, only a few feet away from ending it all. I'll tell you later," said Jensen.

"I see you found Darrow's real name," said Niki.

"Sophie got it, I didn't," said Jensen.

"Come to Jed's farm and see me soon," said Jensen to Sophie and Darrow.

"We will, we're near there hunting often," said Sophie.

"Well what about every market day, we'll meet and visit," said Jensen.

The dragons flew back to their lair and dwarfs looked after their wounded and dead.

"We have to be going now King Harden. I thank you very much for your hospitality and I hope we can talk more about trade when you get things sorted out," said Niki.

They rode home the way they came along the coast.

"Let's not stop off at those creepy ruins on the way," said Jensen.

"You ride the wind on the back of a dragon and you're afraid of ghosts?" said Niki and the others laughed.

# THE GIFTED OF SISCERLY XXVIII
### *The God*

JENSEN CHEERFULLY WALKED DOWN the stairs to Niki's stateroom where Amie and Katie were in hot debate over magic spells.

"Good morning you two and I rule that both of you are wrong," said Jensen.

Katie smiled and watched Jensen clap her hands after speaking as though to get their attention.

She disappeared.

Gone.

Katie looked left, right, behind, and under the desk. She looked at Amie, her eyes wide and mouth open.

"Where did she go?" asked Katie.

"I don't know?" answered Amie.

"Now come on Amie. Is this one of your tricks?" asked Katie.

"No, I swear I have no idea what happened."

"Because if it is, it's not funny any more," said Katie.

"It's not me and I'm starting to worry."

"What do we do?" asked Katie.

"I don't know. I'm still hoping Jensen will reappear laughing at us like it was a joke of some kind."

"Well she's not. What kind of power would it take to snatch a person that way?" asked Katie.

"Nikita can conceal herself but Jensen doesn't have the knowledge to do that. For someone else to move something as complex as a human body, snatch it. I don't know anyone who could do it."

Just then Niki came into the room.

"What's the matter, you two look like you've seen a ghost?" said Niki.

"Jensen's gone, disappeared in front of our very eyes," said Amie.

Niki knew Amie was not one to joke so took her news at face value and wanted it all explained. Amie told every detail from the time Jensen entered the room until she had mysteriously disappeared.

"We have to find her. God knows what's happened to her. Any ideas?" said Niki.

"I'll get Presela, she might be able to find something," said Katie.

Katie went to Presela's room where she sat reading with the help of Cromby her cat.

"I really need your help to find Jensen. I know you've had differences in the past but if your life was on the line she would help you. It's the way she is. So please help me," said Katie.

"Don't be silly we're not the same but we're on the same side. Of course I'll help. Let's go up to Niki's room, I can always get a stronger feeling where a person has last been."

One minute Jensen was talking to Katie and Amie and the next she was standing in this place wherever it was. It was an old building of some kind. Well somebody had to be in charge.

"Hello. Hello. Somebody, anybody."

Nobody answered.

Jensen searched high and low yet found no one save four men made of stone. It appeared to be an old temple or maybe a shrine.

It had only one floor and from what she could see three large rooms. The largest looked like an abandoned place of worship. The first thing to catch her eye was the blood red pentagram. Squares, circles, and pentangles of all sizes cover the floor. Little pictures, runes, were drawn here and there, of what she didn't know. She had seen them before; they were used by witches and sorceresses to cast spells.

This was a place of magic and that's how she got here, a spell of some sort. The only other things in the room were four cracked statues standing at the far end. High ceilings made of decomposing wood hung, sagging, above. The windows were barred and upon checking the front door she found it was locked. Jensen was a prisoner here.

The room on her right looked like some kind of storage room as there was no window at all. It had been converted to a bedroom and was clean but not cosy. Stone walls and the decaying ceiling gave her no sense of warmth. It was a prison, that's all, and it looked as though she was the sole inmate.

The last room was a dining room with a large table surrounded by about twenty chairs. Jensen approached the table and looked close. A freshly cooked meal for about five sat upon it. Steam came from the meat and vegetables; it had just been set.

Jensen jumped when she heard a pop and a snap and saw it came from the hearth; a fire burned fresh logs as though it had just been started.

"Hello, Hello, somebody, anybody."

Nobody.

Dare she touch the food? Why not? Anyone having the power to bring her here this way could kill her whenever he wanted. He wouldn't have to poison her food. Jensen grabbed a few slices of hot turkey and walked toward the window.

Jensen glanced to all sides and spotted an old castle across the courtyard. The whole place was surrounded by crumbling walls with two old rotten gates at one end. They were closed which meant little as an old woman could break them down. The ramparts were only half there, some beams hung ready to fall. The whole place looked as though a weak hurricane would blow the loose rocks across the land and no one would know it had ever existed.

All day long Jensen looked for a way out, some weakness she could take advantage of but found none. The mortar was falling out between the stones but they were too heavy for her to lift. The only door out was almost new and solidly built. It was the only thing of this century in the place; the door that was keeping her in.

Jensen looked toward the castle often hoping to catch a glimpse of someone but never did. The place wasn't deserted as laundry hung on a line strung between the castle and a shed. All was clean and no debris littered the yard. Someone looked after it including the temple she was in.

The sun sank below the castle walls and darkness slowly

replaced light. Jensen lit candles placed throughout the rooms. It was then that she felt as though being watched; felt eyes upon her. Jensen was afraid to look behind her but finally did. With a lump in her throat and a knot in her heart she slowly turned.

No one.

The feeling refused to go away; it gnawed at her like a great looming ghost. She felt more and more aware of it by the minute and turned slowly scanning the room. It was as though there were eyes in all the walls staring at her. Maybe that was it; maybe there were hidden passages with peep holes that her captors were looking through.

Jensen returned to the dining table, sat and swallowed some more meat, trying to look calm. She hid her shaking hands under her arms and held herself tight. What would Katie do now thought Jensen? Katie would always stay calm and look as though she was in command no matter what the situation. If Katie was here in Jensen's place she would appear to be the jailer, not the captive. What would Katie do next? Maybe she would bluff. What would it hurt?

"All right you can come out now whoever you are. I'm not afraid and I know you can hear so whether it be today or tomorrow show yourself. I know you want to take a bow and want me to see the genius who locked me up here," said Jensen.

Jensen fought to stay calm. She was proud of herself as her voice did not waver and she was still reasonably composed.

"Bravo, I knew you had courage when I saw you," said a man who suddenly appeared out of nowhere.

The stranger was tall with a dark complexion and had a thin physique. The man wore a blue silk robe with gold trim.

He had a majestic look about him, confidence in the way he conducted himself. His hair was brown with greying patches here and there. The main thing about the man that gave her a chill was his grey eyes. They gave her the feeling she was being watched even when he turned away.

"Who are you and why have you abducted me?" asked Jensen.

"My name is Mesado. I'm a son of the God of Light and lastly you have not been abducted but are merely my guest."

"Well then I've had a nice visit but have to run. I have kin and a country to save so if you don't mind let me out of here."

"Not so quick young lady we have not yet had the time to get acquainted. Once you get to know me you might not want to leave."

"How did I know you were going to say something like that? So then I'm not a guest but a prisoner, all right. Why me?"

"Because you are an enchantress dear lady, the one and only and I have to have you."

Jensen stood and walked his way then put her hand over his heart.

"Take me back this instant."

"Hah, that is cute. You think your power will work with the Gods. Who do you think gives you these gifts anyway?"

Jensen also had a feeling that would not work but had to try.

"How long do I have to stay?"

"It's not the length of time Jensen as time has no meaning here. You will not grow older and will not change from what you are now."

"You know I can't stand the loneliness for long, our kind can't."

"You will not be lonely my dear, you will have me."

Jensen would get nowhere with him and she knew it so only sat looking down at the food. Jensen couldn't think of a worse predicament to be in; a slave to a God. Who in the world could help her now?

Niki sat at a table leafing through a book, Amie at her side her doing the same. Presela sat holding Cromby reading through her cat's eyes. Cromby kept shifting as he lost interest but Presela managed somehow.

Katie was growing frustrated looking for something, anything to give her a clue. There may be no hint in the old books as to how Jensen disappeared.

Everyone was doing something trying to locate Jensen.

The transparent image of Kenji appeared in the room.

"I've lost touch with Jensen; I can feel her no more. Where is she?"

"She's disappeared," said Katie.

Katie explained every last detail to Kenji who looked as dumbfounded as the others.

Kenji looked deep and thought then finally spoke, "I know of no one capable of doing such a thing. I will return and search the old books. But first let us think this through.

"Who knows the most about wizards and their talents? Who's been around the longest with the power to see? Who has been involved with everyone with the gift? Who is always looking for an edge? Who is the one person you would ask if you wanted to know what we are looking for?" said Kenji.

Everyone looked at each other and knew who she meant but no one wanted to say the name.

Finally Amie let out a sigh and said, "Ises."

"There's no one I'd rather avoid dealing with than her," said Niki.

"You're right though Kenji. We could sit here and read for the next year and not have the knowledge she has of shady people powerful and devious enough to do this," said Katie.

"Getting her to part with what she knows is the problem. She can't be trusted either, not as far as you could throw a horse," said Niki.

Katie stood and said, "Presela and I should go there and find out what we can. Presela because she may be able to read something that Ises is thinking or at least pick up on a lie."

"All right then I'll arrange a ship. It'll take over a week to get there and back," said Niki.

Katie sat down again and looked at the floor in silence as though she'd not heard a word Niki had said. Her friend's life was at stake and so was the future of the country. Katie had to do all she could. Katie still couldn't force herself to say what had to be said. She just sat and stared blank eyed at the floor.

"Are you all right Katie?" asked Niki.

Katie looked at the faces staring at her then turned her eyes back to the floor.

Finally Katie sighed and said, "A boat will take too long."

"How are you going to get there?" asked Niki.

"Dragon."

It was all Katie could get out. There was nothing Katie feared more than heights; she couldn't even climb a tree. Katie looked at Presela whose mouth was open wide. It was the first time Katie had seen expression in her dead eyes; fear stared back at her. Cromby hissed; he finally got the message too.

"Oh no," said Presela, "I don't like Jensen that much."

Katie only smirked and shook her head.

"With that I'll take my leave and find out what I can from my mountain," said Kenji.

The transparent image of Kenji disappeared.

Jensen had arranged to meet Sophie and Darrow in the meadow on Jed's farm every market day. Today was market day. Katie waited, Presela by her side. Out of nowhere two hulking figures swooped from the sky almost colliding with the ground. They levelled, flew on and then quickly returned, landing before Katie and Presela.

Katie had never before in her life trembled with fear, it was not in her nature, until today. She was on the verge of calling it quits but thought of Jensen; her friend would do anything to help her. Katie stared at Presela who was trembling as well. Cromby hissed then sunk deep into her coat.

"Jensen's gone. Disappeared. Can you help us?" said Katie.

Katie repeated her story again the same way as before. Each time Katie repeated it she'd hoped a revelation would come her way that would answer the mystery of Jensen's disappearance.

Sophie listened to every word and seemed to hang on every syllable as though trying to solve the problem herself. Katie knew that dragons had been around for a million years before man had set foot on this earth. If past knowledge could solve their dilemma then it would come from them.

After thinking on it and looking to Darrow for help Sophie finally spoke.

"I can think of no one who could do such a thing. To answer your question though, of course I will help; I'll do anything I can. Jensen's our best friend so just tell me what to do."

"We need to go to the Isle of the Gods. Ises may know something. Can you take us?" said Katie.

"Sure, hop on," said Sophie.

"I'm afraid of heights," said Katie.

"So am I," said Darrow then laughed in that gruff voice of his.

"Climb on and close your eyes. You don't need to see a thing," said Sophie.

Katie climbed on Darrow's waiting shoulder and Presela on Sophie's. They both grabbed a spike and held tight.

"Here we go," said Sophie.

Both Sophie and Darrow crouched then rose to their hind legs at the same time. Great wings spread, raised and beat down. They easily lifted and started to climb.

Jensen had told Katie about her flights with Sophie so Katie came prepared. Katie and Presela dressed for warmth: leather pants, wool coat, mittens, and hat. Katie made the mistake of looking down and almost passed out. Katie looked at Presela; Cromby's head was out of sight so Presela would be flying blind. Lucky girl.

Katie looked left, right and ahead, occasionally glancing down. The more she did it the easier it became, feeling queasy every time but had no fear of passing out. Katie watched Darrow's wings beat and felt every powerful stroke. It was a matter of trust in the dragon and its ability. That was a trait Jensen had; Jensen trusted every one and everything in nature until it let her down, then she'd forgive whatever it was for not being able to cope.

Katie was finally able to look upon the earth below, the horizon, and the sky. It was a beautiful world up high, so much blue and green. Katie couldn't get over how small everything was and how much of everything she could see. The armies of Kamahl were at her right, little tin soldiers like the kind children had as toys. Tiny horses, like the ones on chess boards; the ones Niki's commanders would play. The world was like a map Katie had seen on a table when they were planning war strategies.

The mountains in the distance loomed like jagged peaks but were not as intimidating as from the ground. Katie thought to herself that she could rule the world from up here. But then who would want to? Who would want to take on the suffering of the poor and disabled? Who would want the responsibility of feeding and looking after everyone in the world? Who could listen to the thousands of cries in the night? Only a tyrant or a God. Kamahl was such a tyrant who thought he was a God. Kamahl took what he wanted and destroyed the rest.

Katie believed Niki had the right idea to let people rule themselves. Let individuals help each other. Not be a dictator stealing from the poor for the benefit of the few. It was Niki's dream to let all be free and neighbour help neighbour through bad times and let them share the good. Niki's taxes were small, only enough to support an army to police the country. Her farms paid for her own needs and the castle. Everything seemed so clear from up here and oppressors looked so small.

Land ahead as an island appeared on the distant horizon. In Katie's mind she made plans to land outside the temple grounds and quietly sneak in. She would take Ises and hold her hostage. No one would dare do anything out of turn.

Sophie and Darrow landed directly in the court yard in front of the temple. Darrow roared loud enough to startle everyone making Katie shudder. It seemed as though Sophie and Darrow had their own way of doing things; stealth was not in their books. Katie climbed down from Darrow and met Ises coming from the temple. Soldiers ran toward the dragons, bows in hand.

"Tell your men to take a walk as it would be suicide to shoot an arrow right now," said Katie.

"Well, well. Two dragons this time," Ises said it as though it was a joke.

The woman was more than courageous, she was arrogant and that's one thing Katie could not endure. Katie liked humble country folk not self indulgent people like her. Katie removed her snake belt and turned it into a sword then walked toward the men. Sophie and Darrow who had acted like the soldiers weren't even there turned to face them. Together they roared causing the earth to tremble.

Men were thought to be brave if their courage held; theirs did not. First one man broke rank then a second later a few more. Then they all ran save one, the commander. Katie walked his way as he held out his sword and pointed it her way almost touching Katie's chest. Katie's left hand came up and a flame sprang forth, singeing his sword hand. The commander dropped the weapon and picked it up in his left.

"Stand down you fool, the witch gave you a warning, she won't give you another," said Ises.

The commander dropped his sword and backed away.

"What do you want? What are you doing here?" said Ises.

That arrogance again showed and Katie could take no more. Katie commanded her sword to turn into a snake, a live one at that. Katie held its head and wrapped it around the neck of the Ises. The snake's tongue lashed close to the priestess; one inch closer and it would bite.

"Shut up Ises, all right, I'll do the talking for now. Whenever I need you to say something I'll let you know," said Katie.

Katie saw Ises swallow hard and took it as an agreement of sorts. Katie turned the snake into a belt and tied it around her waist.

"Someone has taken Jensen before our very eyes. You know, like puff, she's gone. Who could and would do a thing like that?" said Katie.

"Mesado," said Ises.

Just like that? Katie thought there had to be more. Ises made no demands, had asked for nothing in return? There was something wrong with that. Besides which Katie knew Mesado from the inn at Sharks Way, a drunk and a dud wizard he was.

"Mesado the creep couldn't pull a dove from a hat," said Katie.

"Mesado can now and more, he's found something, somewhere that's all I know. The dud as you call him is almost as powerful as Kamahl," said Ises.

"And you tell me just like that, you want nothing in return, that's not the Ises we all know," said Katie.

"I told you because he crossed me on an agreement we had, to share knowledge. Mesado is not sharing it. He only gave me a demonstration, took one of the soldiers and brought him back. Mesado himself popped in and out," said Ises.

"Will he turn Jensen over to Kamahl?" asked Katie.

"I don't think so. Mesado is full of himself right now. I don't think he knows what to do with his new found power, wherever it comes from. The man has come upon something big, some knowledge he's stumbled on as that idiot is too stupid to come up with anything on his own. That's all and everything that I know," said Ises.

"Why did he take her? What good will it do?" asked Katie.

"I don't know. Maybe because he could, I really don't know," said Ises.

"Where can I find them?" asked Katie.

"I don't know."

"Ises is lying," said Presela.

"Do you want me to get Sophie to take you for another ride? Jensen said you liked the first one," said Katie.

"Witch Isle but don't tell him I told you so. I don't need that idiot coming after me."

Katie looked at Presela who nodded so she was telling the truth.

The flight back to the mainland was shorter than the one to the island as the wind was behind them all the way. They landed at Jed's farm in the evening. Sophie and Darrow would stay the night and breakfast would be on Katie. Katie and Presela rode back to the castle to arrange a wagonload of meat to be delivered the next morning. The dragons would wait while Katie met with Niki and Amie.

Katie explained everything to them, everything Ises had said.

"So what do we do?" asked Katie.

Niki was deep in thought and Amie flipped through pages in a book. Katie thought she would have to ask the question again as no one had heard it the first time.

Finally Niki spoke, "We'll go to Witch Island, Katie, you and I. We'll see what's going on."

"How are we going to travel?" said Katie already knowing the answer but just wanted to make sure.

"Dragon, I know I'm not looking forward to it," said Niki.

# The Gifted of Siscerly XXIX
## *The Catwoman*

Jensen again searched for a way out but failed. Jensen knew if her stay was any longer she would go insane.

Mesado did his appearing out of nowhere act and joined her.

"Let's go for a walk. I'll show you the castle and we'll have diner there," said Mesado.

The front door opened for him with but a wave of his hand. By the light of a few torches in the courtyard they walked toward the castle. Even in semi darkness Jensen could see that the stones of the courtyard were different colors. There were stones of red shaped like a pentagram and stones of grey in the centre. The whole place was like a wizard's spell. The castle looked to be older than her prison and in need of much repair. A dozen stone masons could spend the next year here and it would still look shabby to her.

"There are cliffs on three sides and only a small beach where fishing boats come and go. Even if you stole a boat you would have to row it for a week to get anywhere. The fishermen know if they help any stranger, well they know they'll die slowly and in pain," said Mesado.

That was not good news; he'd not missed a thing. Jensen was definitely a prisoner here. Mesado left her with only one choice; kill him, simple as that. Jensen still had her dagger but thought to herself he'd not overlooked it. She was no danger to him even armed. She would look for a weakness in the castle and find one if one was there. She doubted that at this moment that he had overlooked anything.

As they approached the castle door an old woman appeared. "Hello Sadie," said Mesado.

She was in chains; another prisoner it seems.

"Sadie's been bad," scoffed Mesado.

They entered the main hall and then went to the dining room. Everything was old and showed signs of wear. Not antique but old and worn out long ago. Not the kind of place a God would live thought Jensen.

They sat at the table and were served by an old woman bent and crippled with age.

"Hello Ellie," said Mesado.

The next sight made Jensen feel ill at ease but she did her best to hide her feelings and disdain. A woman came into the room. The woman looked like a cat. Her eyes were green; she had black hair, and sported a woman like figure. She was a beauty but her eyes were round and piercing, her face oval, and a slight black moustache looked like whiskers. She looked like a cat.

"Hello Marawka," said Mesado.

"Good day."

Jensen saw a look exchanged between the two she had

seen many times before. They were lovers, Mesado and the cat woman.

A rundown castle, one servant in chains, one that could hardly walk, and a woman that looked like a cat. This was no God or even the son of one. They were a band of gipsies at best.

There was something else that hit her as strange. It was small and inconclusive yet sprung to her mind. Mesado had shown himself only in the dark, never in the light of day. Whatever that meant Jensen wasn't sure. He was the son of the God of light. What was that all about? Why didn't he show himself when it was light?

And most of all, if he wasn't a God then why did Jensen's power not work on him? It worked on all men so far to some degree but not on him. Was it some sort of web or ward? Was it some kind of spell? Jensen was immune to magic and her gift took precedence over all. Jensen thought about it then came to a conclusion. There were only three options: he really was a God, he was not a man, or he was dead. Jensen almost ruled out the first and the second was not likely either as he and the cat woman appeared to be mates. That left only the third; he was dead. On the top of her list at this time; she needed to take a look around this creepy place.

"You'll have to show me around your castle, its old and quaint, I love things of age," said Jensen.

Mesado nodded and smiled but the cat woman looked at her like she was dinner to be.

There was only one word that described how Jensen felt about her, weird. Marawka was not human; something nature would not lay claim to.

They went through room after room never escaping the

cat woman's gaze. Then Jensen saw an odd sight; a bedroom with shutters on the inside. There was a chain and a padlock securing them. There were men's clothes in the room. It was Mesado's bedroom and it looked like the son of the God of light hated the sun. They stayed up the night long talking and looking over the castle.

The one place Mesado avoided even though Jensen wanted to see it was the cellar. Mesado was nervous as Jensen reached for the door that led below. The cat woman almost sprang at her throat. There was something down there.

"What are you going to do with me?" asked Jensen.

"I don't know. Whatever takes place," said Mesado.

"Are you going to give me to Kamahl?" asked Jensen.

"It's tempting. He would pay a king's ransom for you and so would Nikita to get you back. At this time you may be an asset to me. I really haven't made up my mind," said Mesado.

As Jensen went through the castle she noticed it was the same as the temple. There were pentagrams, circles, squares, and strange symbols all over the place, in every room. Marawka's cat eyes never left her all night, they were locked in place. It was as though Jensen were being sized up for some event yet to unfold. Jensen paid her no heed, acted as though she wasn't there. That alone seemed to infuriate Marawka and Jensen's special attention to Mesado that night made the cat woman's hair stand on end. They were not going to be friends any time soon.

There was a slight light breaking the horizon; Marawka was the first to notice. Mesado took Jensen back to the temple in haste and left quickly after locking the door. Jensen hated long good byes in any case especially from that creep. Jensen had to find a way out and search the cellar that Mesado avoided.

There was something in there, she could feel it. Jensen felt the edginess in him and the cat woman when she started toward the basement door.

The sun warmed Jensen's heart after a cold night. It looked so clean and new compared to the crumbling walls it rose above. Its bright light showed age all around something that had outlived its time. Even the gray trees in the courtyard were knarred and leafless, devoid of life. They too were refusing to lie down.

Jensen frantically looked for a way out in every room, in every corner but found nothing. Mesado had left her dagger. Had he nothing to fear or was it an oversight? No, Mesado simply had nothing to fear. He was as arrogant as any man could be; overconfident or immortal, one of the two.

Jensen dug and scraped at the bars in a window facing the rear. The old mortar reluctantly gave way but finally did to the blue blade. She lifted the bars out of the window opening and set them on the ground.

The sun was at its highest point of the day; it was noon as Jensen scurried across the courtyard to the castle. She tried the front door. It squeaked open, thanks be the Gods it wasn't locked. Jensen closed it behind her and listened but heard not a sound. They were probably all creatures of the night and now asleep.

Down to the cellar Jensen went as there was no lock on the door. She found a candle and flint to light it then looked around. There were dozens of books written with pen and quill, none labelled or signed. Jensen leafed through them and found diagrams and symbols she'd seen on the ground. The castle was laid out in drawings and print. What did it all mean?

Jensen looked and studied then found a name that often came up, Archadies. It was the name Amie had mentioned of a wizard, a thousand years old but fantasy or so Amie claimed. Archadies was the brunt of many a folklore and tales told to children to invoke fear at night. What if he was real?

Jensen looked at the pentagrams, drawings, and text and came to a conclusion; the whole place was magic waiting to be invoked. Certain words spoken in the right place would bring things about. What exactly Jensen wasn't sure. The books on the table she left in place but there were some in shelves covered with dust that had not been touched in a while. Jensen took two and started to climb the cellar steps.

Jensen had an eerie feeling, something was amiss. She pinched out the candle and squinted through a crack in the old cellar door. There was a huge black cat walking about. It was the size of Marawka. And that's exactly who it was; she could feel it. The cat made its way down the hall then upstairs. Jensen slowly opened the door and tip toed out of the castle, her heart beating like a drum.

Across the courtyard and into the room Jensen had left a short time ago. She set the bars back into place and swept away the dust from where she'd dug it out. Then into her bedroom Jensen ran eager to decipher the two books she'd taken.

It was Archadies alright and his magic filled every corner of the place. Pentagrams and symbols were set up in advance to perform certain tasks. One in the temple main room could move a person from place to place which is exactly how she was abducted. That's also the way Mesado popped in and out.

Book two frightened Jensen to no end but explained everything about the cat woman and Mesado's night habits. Archadies was experimenting with the human body to create walking weapons. With one spell he could change a man into a beast of the night that lived off the blood of others. A weapon by its very nature was meant to destroy by surviving off the lives of the enemies it was set upon. Archadies had created beasts that were half men and half wolf depending on the light of the moon; powerful weapons that could be created from the neighbour next door.

These walking weapons were almost immortal and were self replicating. Their traits would show up in the next generation creating an endless chain. The spell could also be passed to another by a bite while feeding off the victim's blood. The victim would die but come to life again. The victim would turn into another hunter of blood. A stake through the heart was the only way to kill one. That or tie one up out in the sun. Sensitivity to sunlight was an acceptable trade off for ones as powerful as these, so written by Archadies.

Jensen thought about family members having to kill an infected kin. That would be too much for her to bear.

Jensen also found the cat woman spell creating a beast that would protect his night legions during the day; someone to watch over his creations. She felt that Archadies thought he was a God. Now Mesado did as well.

There was only one problem with all that he created. The creatures were impossible to control. They fought amongst themselves and could not be depended upon to follow the cause of man. They were not enticed by gold or material wealth. They were as created; these creatures lived for the blood of man. Their single purpose was to survive and live off the death of others. They owed no allegiance to any man even the one that gave them life.

It was a useless experiment into the realms of the unknown,

even beyond the world of the dead. It was a nightmare created by a man who was too powerful and wise for his own good. And the good of the world that gave him life.

How could anyone totally ignore the past, their parents and all their kin? How could anyone turn against the origins of man? Who was self indulgent enough to recreate the world? Who had the right to meddle with the nature of man?

Jensen found answers in the text. Archadies left the castle one night to destroy a half wolf, half man that threatened him. No more entries were logged. The wolf man won. Archadies created a world no one would want; no one could cope with, even the Keeper of the Dead. It was a world devoid of reason or the values of life. It was a world of chaos among creatures not meant to walk this earth. It was a world no one wanted. It was thrust onto them by a man of distorted vision who sought to perfect life above what the Gods had derived.

It was the world of those not alive yet not dead, a world of those not yet departed.

So Mesado came upon this castle and stumbled onto the books and presto a super wizard was born. He'd used one of the body transformation spells on himself and another on Marawka. They were both almost immortal, almost. Jensen now knew why her power did not work on him as he was not really alive. Mesado was not of the underworld either so her destructive power did not turn him to dust. Mesado and Marawka were from a world of itself, a world not of life or death that would never meld into either. No God or Keeper had dominion over the two; that alone would be enticing to some.

Night came too quickly for Jensen as the sun sank into the horizon and was replaced by an almost full moon. With the night came Mesado and his silly grin. He was so sure of himself as though he had made himself into a God. Mesado was a fool that stumbled on a recipe for disaster and didn't know it or maybe didn't care. The man gave her the chills like never before, now knowing what he really was.

"Let's go for a walk, it's a quiet evening," said Mesado.

"Why not, I have nothing else to do thanks to you," said Jensen.

"Your mouth is going to get you into trouble someday," said Mesado.

"Even if it's the truth?"

"Especially when it's the truth," said Mesado.

They walked across the courtyard and out the front gate to the fields beyond the castle walls.

"Aren't you afraid I'll run away," said Jensen.

"Where to?"

"The village and then over the sea," said Jensen.

"The villagers fear me they would just bring you back and if not. Remember how you got here in the first place. I could just bring you back again," said Mesado.

Jensen knew that was the painful truth. In saying it he'd just declared that one of the two had to die. She wasn't going to live with him and he wasn't about to let her go. "Till death do us part," was the way they put it at weddings and that's the way it was with them now. Jensen hoped it would be him that wound up dead and not her. She had to think of a way to get him out in the sun. That or drive a wooden stake through his heart which he wouldn't let her do.

Jensen was so tired not having slept at all during the day and would now have to cater to him all night.

"I'm not used to sleeping during the day. That would take some getting used to," said Jensen.

"Oh you'll acquire a taste for it as did I once you become one of us," said Mesado.

That hit Jensen in the face like a dirty shovel. Mesado was going to turn her into a walking beast like him. No way. But then he knew all the spells; just say the right words in the right place over her and she would be one of the walking dead. That or bite her and feed from her life's blood. Jensen had to get out of this fast; tomorrow at the latest; if she lasted that long.

That night was a struggle to survive but fear of what he could do kept her awake. Jensen was careful never to stand within a pentagram or a circle as a spell would mean the end of life as she knew it. The cat woman was hardly ever there making Jensen wonder what was going on between the two. As soon as she was brought back to the temple sleep overcame her.

Jensen woke and rushed to see where the sun was so she would have an idea of the time. It was afternoon and she cursed herself for falling asleep. She pulled out the bars and grabbed the books she'd taken the previous day then raced toward the castle. Jensen exchanged the books for two more and snuck out the cellar. At the front door she had an idea.

Jensen set the books on the floor and walked toward the stairs. She quietly went up one step at a time trying to avoid making them squeak. She made her way to Mesado's door and turned the lever. It was locked. She snuck back downstairs and around the corner toward the front door finding herself nose to nose with Sadie.

"Shh," hissed Sadie and grabbed her arm then led her out the front door.

"You trying to get killed?" said Sadie.

"I'm dead anyway if I stay here," said Jensen.

"Go back to the temple before Marawka sees you."

"Are you going to tell?"

"No child, I'd like to help. I'd be happy to be away from that pair. She's a killer four times over that I know of and so is he. I am the keeper here and they came for help one night and never left. They found the books and learned some spells that turned them both into beasts," said Sadie.

"Can you get me the key to his room for tomorrow?"

"Yes. What are you going to do?" asked Sadie.

"Make him go away, I hope. See you tomorrow Sadie."

Jensen grabbed the books and returned to the temple for a busy afternoon of reading. At least she'd gotten some much needed sleep that morning and most of all help.

# The Gifted of Siscerly XXX
## *To Fight a God*

On the island where Jensen was a captive of the Son of a God and a cat woman, she lay on her bed reading. She memorized spells for the rest of the day and well into the night. Then the self proclaimed Son of God, Mesado, came.

"You have given me nothing in return for my hospitality so far," said Mesado.

"I won't thank you for abducting me if that's what you want," said Jensen.

"Sooner or later of your own free will you will give yourself to me. Time is on my side not yours, so why wait if you are to be mine in any case," said Mesado.

"If time is on your side then what's the hurry." said Jensen and it seemed to stop Mesado cold.

"Let's go for a walk," said Mesado.

They did the same thing that night as the night before. Jensen feigned a headache so Mesado took her back to the temple earlier than usual. It wasn't only the headache (as he didn't really care what she felt like) but also the fact that

Marawka clung to him all night long. The cat woman wanted some private times with him as jealousy of Jensen set in more and more every day.

Sadie came to her back window shortly after her return with a key in her hand.

"It's a spare key; they don't know I have it. If you do something then do it fast. He sent a fisherman to Kamahl the wizard to tell him you were here. You were to be for him from the start but he wanted you for himself for a while. Marawka has been pushing him to rid himself of you," said Sadie.

"All right, what I do will be done today at first light, one way or another it will end then," said Jensen.

Jensen sat at the window facing the east, holding the key tight to her chest in both hands. Jensen prayed to all the Gods she'd ever heard of for a bright sun. She must have missed one as the sun rose almost hidden from view behind steely grey clouds.

In the mist Jensen snuck to the castle and through the front door. She spotted the big cat before it saw her. She ran to the cellar door and hid behind it at the top of the stairs. Through a crack she watched the cat as it lay near the foot of the stairs.

Jensen found the candle and flint; lit the candle and decide to make use of her time. Jensen leafed through the old books and found more spells. Her head hurt from cramming things into memory. Some of the first things she'd learned were becoming a muddle. She was mixing one spell with another; it was too much and would do her no good.

Jensen snuck to the top of the cellar stairs. The cat was still there. And old chute for dropping fire wood into the cellar was big enough for her to climb out. The first thing she saw that warmed her heart was the sun burning away the fog. It was almost visible; one of those Gods had heard her prayer.

Jensen was outside the castle and knew that a distraction was needed. She found it in the way of and empty rain barrel. The courtyard was on a slight grade toward the wall so that rainwater could run away from the castle. Jensen rolled the barrel with a mighty push; it rolled toward the wall. She jumped down the shoot and landed in the cellar hearing a mighty crash as the barrel slammed into the castle wall. Up the stairs Jensen ran. The big cat was gone.

Jensen pulled the key from her trousers and ran up the stairs to Mesado's room. She fumbled with the lock and it finally gave way. She closed the door behind her in case the cat returned. Mesado lay in a bed almost completely surrounded by curtains. She peeked; it was him alright, tight asleep.

Jensen raced to the window and pried at the lock with her dagger. The lock stood fast but the old bolts holding the rusty latch gave way. The inside shutters were open. There were outside shutters as well. She grabbed and old chair and with all her strength slammed it into through the glass and into the wooden barriers. They held fast.

A hand on Jensen's shoulder pulled her away and she turned to see Mesado with fangs. Jensen ducked sliding away under his grip and ran toward the door. There was a growl outside. It was the cat. She drew the dagger and rushed toward Mesado but at the last second ducked under his arm. She raced toward the window her body slamming against the shutters. They gave way. She flew out the broken window.

Jensen snatched a grip of the window ledge on the way out and held herself, not even trying to move. Before she could look down to see the trouble she was in Mesado appeared in the window his top teeth exposed. Mesado stared down at her raising a hand to strike then noticed the smoke coming from his chest. Before he could react Jensen reached and grabbed one of his hands only an inch away. Jensen reached up with the other hand and held his one hand in both of hers as he tried to pull away. She tugged and tugged to keep him in the sunlight. Mesado smoked more and more as screams of agony came from within him. The skin of his hand was hot and starting to come loose so she grabbed the window ledge again. Mesado screamed and fell to the floor out of sight. One last shriek and he was silent; he sounded like a screaming child.

Jensen looked down, her arms were aching, begging for her to let go. Two floors up, she could break a leg on the cobblestone below. She still had the cat woman to contend with and that would not be an easy task. She could not muster the strength to climb back into the room. Her arms and hands were screaming for relief.

It was then she saw a heart warming sight as Sadie and Ellie raced her way with a ladder. They'd been watching all the time. Jensen heard a smashing sound from inside and knew it was the door. A cat's black head appeared, fangs bared. A ladder slammed against the wall at her right. Jensen jumped as the black tiger's claw slashed at her grip. She half slid half climbed to the bottom of the ladder. Her body ached but she had no time to assess damages.

"Thank you but now you must run and hide. There's no telling what the cat woman will do. Run. Run," said Jensen.

Jensen watched them leave then jumped into the chute and landed in the cellar. Oh, that felt anything but good. Her body hurt so much she wanted to cry. No time for crying now.

Jensen found the candle and flint and struck it again and

again. Her hands were so sore and would hardly move as she dropped the flint over and over again. Finally it started and she heard a roar from above then saw a black shape blot out the sun in the chute. Jensen raced to retrieve a torch from the wall and with a hiss it broke into a flame. She blew out the candle and with the torch in hand raced up the cellar steps. Before she reached the top the big cat was in the cellar and chasing her. Jensen heard its roar and could feel its hot breath at her heels.

Jensen made it to the top of the stairs and slammed the door. A mighty thud sounded a second later and the old door almost gave way. She braced it with her back as another thud shook her body and the door. That thing was strong. She knew what was coming and shivered at the thought.

Jensen finally told herself to breath as not a sound was to be heard. She knew the big cat was gone. It had jumped back up the chute and was outside. Lucky for her the front door was closed and locked. Jensen had time to form a plan.

Glass flew to her left as a black shape leapt through the window. Jensen's dagger came out of the sheath as she lunged at the big cat with the torch as a shield. It was big, bigger than she thought; it was bigger than her. The torch held it at bay but the cat grew braver and pawed at it trying to knock it from Jensen's hand.

Jensen's plan was not to kill it as she didn't have the strength for that. She wanted to move it right over a pentagram filled with symbols of who knows what. She'd seen them in the book and knew only that with them stood a chance. Jensen was starting to weaken as the cat got nearer, its claws almost striking home. Then over the pentagram it moved.

Jensen uttered the words she'd seen in the books, "Tether,

rope, or chain will not stop me from turning you into a goat," said Jensen.

"Bah," she heard instead of a growl.

The same spell that turned her into a beast in the first place turned her into a goat. So eager was Marawka to seek revenge for Mesado that she forgot what was there or maybe didn't think Jensen knew. Jensen knew.

The goat ran from the torch. She opened the front door and it raced out. Jensen crawled upstairs to Mesado's room. She had to know for sure. Mesado was dead as any man or beast could be; burned beyond recognition; only ashes remained.

Jensen crawled down the stairs to the waiting arms of Sadie and Ellie. They helped her to the kitchen and sat her in a chair. Both tended her wounds, fussed, and cried.

"Oh dear Missy thank you so much for what you've done. You could have died ten times over," cried Sadie.

Jensen couldn't even nod as her body hurt so much. She wasn't built like Katie, wasn't meant to jump from windows or fight tigers. Jensen was slim and easily hurt. She never played ball games like the other girls on Sunday picnics. She always lost or got a bloody nose. Jensen had enough; she was glad it was over.

# THE GIFTED OF SISCERLY XXXI
## *The Prisoner*

THERE WAS A BANG on the front door. Ellie went to answer and soon returned.

"There are four female warriors wishing to see Mesado in the front room. I told them they'd have to wait. I don't think they're the waiting kind. I think they want you Jensen. I think they're from Kamahl," whispered Ellie.

"They're Koto-Ris. Is there a way off the castle grounds from here," asked Jensen.

Sadie clutched Jensen's arm, "I'll get you out of here, and you Ellie, don't even try to stall, show them to Mesado. Like you said they're not the waiting kind and Ellie don't even try to be brave, old girl."

Jensen followed Sadie out of the kitchen to the rear of the castle. They worked their way to a door set in the castle wall. It was old and groaned as they forced it open. They shut it behind them and entered the woods beyond the castle walls.

There was a trail that Sadie told Jensen was used when gathering herbs and things the forest had to offer. Sadie and

Ellie found honey on occasion if they were quick and the bees slow. Mushrooms and berries were plentiful at the right time of the year. Nuts and apples were also retrieved and stored in the cellar in time for the winter snows.

The plan was to make their way to the village and hire a fisherman to take Jensen to Tyhton. Now that Mesado and cat woman were dead the fishermen would have nothing to fear. That was the plan.

Not far from the castle they heard a scream, it was Ellie. They both stopped and turned.

Jensen sunk to her knees, "No, oh please no, I've had enough, please don't kill any more of my friends, I've had enough."

Sadie wrapped her arms around Jensen, "Dear child, it's not your fault, I told her not to try to be brave because I knew she would. Ellie would never betray anyone especially someone like you. She'd probably refused to tell them where you went. It was her gift to you. Don't let her sacrifice be in vain. Do whatever you can. We have to go."

Jensen followed Sadie to the village where they tried to hire a boat. Jensen offered gold coins but no one believed Mesado was dead. The son of a God could not be killed and if he was the Gods would be offended and strike at the ones who would aid the assassins. No one would help. She was on her own.

"Good bye Sadie. You're the best friend a person could ever have. I love you so much and when I'm free I'll return. For now I'm going to steal a boat and believe me in the world of men I can," said Jensen.

They hugged then Jensen went to the first boat she saw and told the owner to stand down. He did just that. She wanted nothing more; she would not command anyone to help her and risk death. She was on her own.

Jensen raised the sail blocking out the setting sun as a wind took her to who knows where. She didn't have a clue as to where she was going or how to sail a boat. She had to escape those warrior women; she'd almost died battling one before. Now there were four carrying weapons coated with poison. A touch of a blade would mean certain death.

The night was long and empty on the open sea. She'd planned to keep a shoreline in view but it didn't work out that way. She couldn't see one and late in the night all the lights went out. She'd stowed lots of rations aboard despite her haste. It didn't take a genius to know lack of fresh water would mean death in this world of salt water, the sea. She could be heading out to where no land existed and drift aimlessly until her rations ran out.

Morning came with the news that there was no land in sight. Jensen was sure that even the sun was laughing at her. This was as low as her life could get. She needed to save her family and here she was out in the middle of the sea.

Hope rushed into Jensen's heart at the sight of a large sailing ship closing on her tiny craft. She watched, fingers crossed, longing for a friendly ship. Maybe it was a Tyhton war vessel or a trader belonging to Niki's fleet. Whatever it was closed quickly on her little fishing boat. The sails grew large, four at least coming her way. Closer and closer the ship came not slowing at all. Jensen could make out the woman carved into the ship's bow. She was not smiling, only a solemn look that said, "get out of my way". Jensen saw every detail of the bow. Crash. She was in the sea fighting to stay above the watery deep. She'd never learned to swim.

Someone dove in and strong hands pulled her to safety. She spit salty water onto the deck and looked into the eyes of her saviours. Women clad in leather with weapons at their belt: swords, war axes, and knives. They were Koto-Ri, born and raised to kill.

They all smiled as at last the catch that Kamahl sought was in their grasp.

"Tie her hands and blindfold her. There are sailors aboard. She'll get us all killed if you don't keep an eye on her," said the leader.

Two warriors tied her hands cutting off the flow of blood. They blindfolded her tightening the knot until it felt like a rock pushing against the back of her head.

"Angel is this alright," said one of the women.

Angel was one of Kamahl's commanders. Jensen knew that much of her; she'd seen her before when she kicked her in the face. Angel checked the blindfold and roughly pulled it farther down.

"No, it's not good enough. Don't underestimate this little girl or you'll die," said Angel.

Jensen sat listening; making use of whatever senses she had. She could hear, feel, and smell; she wasn't finished yet. Jensen listened to a sailor and focused on him, on his voice and position. Over and over she said in a whisper that no one could hear, "My mind to your mind, listen to me."

The man stopped talking but she sensed he'd not moved.

"Kill the woman next to me, she's a threat to us all," whispered Jensen.

With a surge she'd experienced before Jensen felt the connection take. The man walked their way; she could hear his feet move across the deck. The Koto-Ri next to her wailed in pain then crashed to the deck. The sailor's agonizing scream was next being heard then a splash in the water told her that the man had been tossed overboard. Jensen didn't care; they were enemies and she would use one against the other until they were all gone.

It felt like a log hit her in the side of the head causing her to tumble to the deck.

"I owed you that enchantress. Now get her below. Do you see what I mean? Minka's dead because she didn't watch herself around her. Don't make the same mistake. Take her below and kill any man that approaches you," said Angel.

"Now listen to me Jensen and listen well. You're alive because you're worth ten thousand gold coins that way and only five if you're dead. If you pull a stunt like that again I'll kill you and suffer the cost, understand?" said Angel.

Angel kicked her twice then sent her with the other two below.

It took forever to reach port as every agonizing moment the ropes burned her wrists and the knot in the blindfold felt like a rock trying to shatter her skull. Jensen prayed for a storm but none came and if one had she would probably drown. They finally reached port, the ship slamming into the dock. There was a cheer and a rush as the sailors abandoned ship racing to the inn near the waterfront.

Jensen was taken from the ship and rudely thrown into the back of a wagon. All three women were strong and treated her with less respect than any man ever would. They kicked, slapped, and punched her whenever they could. Jensen would kill all three if she got the chance.

A long wagon ride ended at sundown; she could see light fading even through her blindfold. There were no men around so there was no need for the blindfold and ropes. There was not and ounce of humanity between the three. They were all heartless and empty as sea shells.

Jensen was led down a busy street, too busy for her to zero in on anyone. She was taken into a building full of people, too full for her to single out an individual man. Her gift was of little use to her blindfolded and in a crowd, hands tied.

Jensen was finally slammed into a bench and told to stay. She dared not move as there was a hand at her throat and a knife at her side. Jensen guessed that they were close to Kamahl now, too close to chance letting her get away. Minutes later she was dragged into a room and stood between two of the women warriors.

"Well, well. If it isn't Jensen. I've been wanting to have a chat with you for quite a while. Oh, I'm sorry about the blindfold and ropes but we don't want you to do anything silly do we?

"Oh, I'm sorry; I've been rude and not introduced myself. I'm Kamahl. I'm sure you've heard of me. I'd like to take you to dinner but I'm rather busy at this time, perhaps tomorrow, I'm sure you understand. I have reserved a room for you in the cellar. It's not much as we're rather cramped at this time. Due to the war you know. I'll enjoy seeing you another day though, I've something special planned. Ladies take her to her room."

Jensen was led downstairs to a stuffy humid cellar. The smell of urine and faeces was thick in the air. A man screamed and groaned as other men laughed at his pain. It was a dungeon.

Jensen was taken to a cell and locked in; hands tied and blindfold still in place. She could have felt sorry for herself; it wouldn't have been hard to do. But she didn't. Jensen concentrated, listened, and separated voices trying to lock minds with the right man.

Mira saw three Koto-Ris take Jensen into Kamahl's castle. Mira was not going to let that last for long. She had to free her.

Mira had been visiting some friends of hers and had been here for several days. After aiding Presela's escape there was a sizable price on her head. Kamahl would love to get his hands on her. But a little paint on her face, a new hat and clothes and no one, not even her friends recognized her. Besides which she was a witch and witches could make people forget certain things. Mira would not let Emperor Kamahl (or whatever he called himself today) stand between her and friends.

Mira had known Kamahl since he was a young man. Kamahl made his way knocking out drunks in alleys to steal their money. He was still a thief today but on a larger scale. Kamahl tried to steal from the wrong man one night, a powerful wizard. The wizard took him into his service instead of killing him which he should have done. The wizard thought Kamahl had spunk and taught him everything he knew; taught him a thousand ways to kill a man. Kamahl used the knowledge to put an end to the old wizard; took his castle and his lands. Kamahl's next victims were the king and all his heirs. With no one to lay claim to the throne Kamahl did and killed all who opposed him.

Mira was on her way to the inn for ale when she spotted Jensen but this would not be the night for drink. Mira went to the stable where she kept her horse Chimneysweep, to line up another one. She had no intention of buying one; she'd not bought a horse yet; stole them all she did; all from the commanders of Kamahl. Mira had to get one sorted out for later tonight. She found a good looking grey, breeding second to none, in a Lord's stall.

And now for a couple of grey robes, the kind the kitchen staff wore, one for her and one for Jensen once she freed her. A friend worked in the kitchens so she knew exactly where to get a couple of those. Mira dressed in the grey uniform that the servants wore and grabbed a pail of the brown slop that they served to Kamahl's special guests in the cellar below.

Down to the dungeons Mira went. This time of night there would be only a few guards, the rest would be eating at the inn. Once inside she made her way along the cells as men grabbed at her for food.

An insistent guard called for her to stop but she ignored the silly man and walked on. Mira acted like she was deaf. Finally at the end of the aisle was Jensen's cell. Mira raised her hand and with a chant, a bang, and a puff of smoke the door flew open. She stepped into the cell after putting out a pesky guard. Mira cut Jensen's ropes and tore the blindfold from her head. By now there were four guards bearing down on them.

"Do your thing Jensen," said Mira.

They were close so Jensen touched two on the chest and commanded them to stop the other two. Their bodies shook and their eyes went wide then glazed as though in another world. Her gift worked as always and a fight broke out between the men. Two more guards joined in as well and it was soon out of control, the way out was open to them.

"I have to find Kamahl. I can end it all tonight if I can get to him," said Jensen.

"He's left, for where I don't know," said Mira.

Jensen slipped a grey servants robe over her travelling

clothes and followed Mira out of the castle. They made their way to the stable. And who was there saddling a horse? Angel.

Angel's sword was out and she raced their way with a blood curdling scream. Mira's hand came up with a wave and the sword was knocked from the Koto-Ri's hand. It was quickly replaced with a war axe that she threw. Mira barely ducked the lightning fast blade which jammed itself into the wall. Angel drew a knife and with another wave of her hand Mira jammed the Koto-Ri's own blade into the warrior's chest. With a gasp of pain the warrior went to her knees. She wasn't dead yet but soon would be, poisoned by her own blade.

Mira had already saddled both horses so they were off before Angel could scream. At the gate Jensen's gift over the soldiers granted them leave. They rode fast through the night no one in pursuit but they knew soon would be. Jensen had escaped and heads would roll if they didn't get her back.

At daybreak they stopped in a clearing not far from the main road. Their horses were in need of water and rest. Soldiers rode by and were probably searching for the two. They could no longer travel the main roads.

It was tough going through the woods and the streams, sometimes fences and dense bush got in their way. They were finally stuck in fields all around and no forests to hide them. They were spotted by a patrol on the edge of the woods.

Jensen and Mira raced through the fields pursued by a pack of soldiers and were riding into the arms of hundreds more. A cloud blotted out the sun as a shadow engulfed Jensen. A great set of claws snatched Jensen from the back of her horse. They were gentle claws and not the killing kind.

"Sophie," yelled Jensen, "Am I ever glad to see you girl."

Jensen reached up and held tight to Sophie's claws. She looked to her right and saw Darrow clutching Mira; the old girl was scared out of her mind. Jensen smiled trying to put her at ease. Mira was definitely the heroine of the day.

Jensen and Mira were set gently down in a field as the dragons hovered above them, and then landed. It was Katie and Presela on board. Jensen half helped, half forced Mira onto Darrow behind Katie then climbed on Sophie behind Presela and they were off. Two great beasts rose into the sky flying over an army sent to capture them. They would not be caught today.

They landed in Jed's field where Jensen hugged Sophie and Darrow. Jensen gave them a kiss then hugged Katie and Presela as well. She tried to wrap her arms around Mira but the old witch was too fast and backed off.

Mira was not the hugging kind.

"I'll buy you an ale whenever I get a chance," said Jensen.

"Now would be a good time for that especially after that ride in the clouds," said Mira.

They all laughed including Mira.

"How did you find us?" asked Jensen.

"After you cleared the island I started to sense you again. Your signals were really strong when you and Mira were together. I saw double images of the same place from different angles through both of your eyes. It wasn't hard," said Presela.

It wasn't hard thought Jensen as Presela again downplayed her precious gift.

They all took a wagon to the castle and had a feast while Mira raced to the inn.

"Where's Niki?" asked Jensen.

"Niki and I went to the island. She stayed to check out the books and the magic of Archadies. Niki thinks there maybe something useful she can use against Kamahl," said Katie.

"Oh no, I saw it first hand. It's all tainted, there's no good in any of it. It can't be controlled. We have to go there and destroy it all. If Kamahl got a hold of it we'd be killed in our sleep by creatures of the night," said Jensen.

Sophie and Darrow were glad to take them to Witch Island in return for breakfast of a few sides of beef.

Jensen noticed the dragons were becoming good friends of Jed and his wife. The farmer had told Jensen he felt safe with the dragons around.

At noon that day they reached the island. Sadie greeted them; Jensen hugged her friend and they talked for a time. Niki was in the cellar studying the books Jensen wanted to burn.

Jensen sat beside Niki and said hello.

"It's of no use Niki. You can't control it. Even Archadies couldn't handle his mad creations. Look at his last entry. He was going out to destroy a beast, half wolf, half man. There are no more entries after that. Can't you see Niki?" said Jensen.

"There's some powerful magic here and you want me to destroy it?" said Niki.

"What happens when Kamahl's spies get this stuff back to him? You know if you take it back to the castle that will happen. You won't use it if it's not safe but he will. Destroy it Niki or it will destroy us all," said Jensen.

The next day Jensen convinced Sadie to leave the island and come back to Siscerly and live with them. With Ellie gone she would be lonely here but at the castle she would find new friends. Jensen would send a ship as soon as she returned then waited for Niki.

"I'm going to stay here with Sadie and wait for the ship and look over the books until then. Maybe I can use some of it indirectly," said Niki.

Jensen knew how much Niki loved her land and would do anything to keep it free. She knew how tempting it must be to harness the magic here and use it against Kamahl. But that would be blight on the land and maybe the world.

"You will destroy it when you leave, won't you Niki?" said Jensen.

"Oh yes, I will, don't worry Jensen," said Niki.

Jensen was still worried Niki wouldn't destroy the tainted spells. Bad things used for the good of the land might one day be the end of man. It was Jensen's main concern. She'd seen Mesado and Marawka; Niki had not.

# The Gifted of Siscerly XXXII
## *The Final Battle*

JENSEN RODE BISCUIT TOWARD Cambells Cross and the river. She stood on a hill overlooking the standoff. The wizard's soldiers on one side and the Princess's troops on the other. Jensen stared toward the hills and saw a gap where a mountain pass lay. Down this pass would come more men in aid of the wizard overrunning their army then Tyhton would no longer be free. Jensen saw Amie talking to a captain below and rode to join her.

"Good morning Amie," said Jensen.

"Good morning to you, you're looking well."

"I came to see the pass," said Jensen.

"They're on their way."

"We have to stop them," said Jensen.

"Niki said she'd take care of that."

"How?"

"I don't know exactly. You have to concentrate on the wizard. Find a way touch the man."

"I will. I'll be ready the day of the battle."

Jensen returned to the castle with Amie, a lot on her mind. She didn't know exactly how she was going to approach the wizard. Kamahl would have Koto-Ri at his side and archers within his ranks. An arrow through her heart would end her life the same as any one else. She grew tired of thinking and jumped into bed. She'd been given her own bedroom within the palace. How about that for the little redhead from Cambells Cross she thought then fell asleep.

The next morning Jensen awoke, the noise of people talking, yelling, and running by her door. She dressed and climbed the stairs to Niki's stateroom. It was full of people, high ranking officials of her staff and the army. Amie saw Jensen and walked her way.

"The wizard's reinforcements are here. The battle is no longer in the future. We fight today."

"I'll get ready."

Jensen rushed to Katie's room and found her already dressed. They both ran to the stable for their horses and rode to the river. They stood at the rear of the troops looking over the battleground. Amie and Niki were soon there.

"I will ride to the mountain pass and block his reinforcements," said Niki.

"They'll attack you as soon as you cross the bridge," said Jensen.

"They won't see me."

With that said Niki pushed her horse toward the bridge. She was wearing pure white and riding a pure white stallion, her blonde hair flowing in the wind. Jensen wondered how a sight like that would not be seen.

She disappeared, was no longer there.

Jensen could not believe her eyes and searched everywhere looking for some sign of the princess.

Niki rode across the bridge into the heart of enemy lines. No soldier reached for the reins, swung a sword, or threw a spear. Not a single soldier looked her way as the spell she'd cast made her invisible to all. Niki rode between wagons and rows of archers toward the mountain pass where reinforcements came their way. Niki would have to stop them or at least slow them if she could, her army was already outnumbered and any more would bring defeat upon them.

It was the way Kamahl conquered countries using great numbers instead of tact. The war wizard would order great hordes to attack and cared not for the loss of lives even on his own side. As long as he vanquished and seized more land that was his only goal.

Niki pushed her mount up the mountain side as far as he could go then climbed to a cliff overlooking the road. Niki didn't have long to wait; they were almost below her riding through a gap between the two mountain faces. The sorceress summoned her power using great energy blasts to send huge rocks crashing their way. In little time the road was blocked and mounted troops could no longer advance toward the battlefield. The foot soldiers however climbed the ridge she'd created so Niki rained rocks on them. Crushed bodies lay on the valley floor but it didn't discourage the endless line of men coming her way. They feared the wizard's wrath more than possible death at her hands.

Niki reached higher on the mountain face and using her gift pried great boulders free causing them to roll turning into an avalanche. The gap in the valley was sealed; no one else would cross.

Niki was drained.

A golden disk appeared in the sky, the wizard's apparition. Niki knew she would never leave the mountain side. She looked at her rings, her power source, dim and lifeless. Niki mind linked to Amie and said good bye. The wizard was here and she'd be dead in minutes. Niki asked Amie to help Jensen; it was all up to that little girl.

Niki had told Jensen that she would destroyed Archadies castle and all his magic. She had not. Well his castle, but then it was ready to fall down in any case. She had not destroyed the books. There was just too much potential within those volumes. Niki had used some of his destructive spells to bring down part of this mountain. The problem was she had to be close to see the ledges and cracks in order to direct the magic. And now the wizard was bearing down on her.

Kamahl would never confront her while she was strong. And why should he? He could use the superior numbers of his army to defeat any power in the world. So why risk a confrontation he could lose?

Kamahl had seen Niki laid waste to his reinforcements and block the only access valley between their two lands. The wizard would know she was drained and would be furious at what she'd done. Niki knew he would come after her before she came to this mountainside. It would be a battle between a strong wizard and a spent sorceress; Niki had no chance at all. That's why the coward was here.

And there was that golden disk in the sky; that seeing all disk; his eyes and ears where only the Gods and eagles exist. He would soon send lightning bolts to destroy her.

Niki had enough power for her last transformation. She would use one of Archadies' spells to change herself into something else; something that would have a chance of surviving the wizard's wrath on the side of this mountain. The problem was, it would be a one way trip, no way back.

Niki dove from the mountain side to the valley thousands of feet below. She had painted the pentagram and appropriate symbols on her body before she left. She chanted the words in Archadies book and hoped that all would work. She felt something; a change within.

Niki transformed into a hawk.

Niki's clothes fell as she escaped them and her rings dropped to the ground. She beat her wings slowly only wanting to break her fall. Lightning bolts shot by her and exploded on the valley walls. Niki wove to avoid a hit and beat her wings to avoid crashing to the valley floor below. Upward she flew and soared first left then right as lightning bolts streamed aimlessly by.

Niki only needed to escape this valley. The wizard would never be able to tell her apart from other hawks. Lightning bolts no longer came her way so she turned to look for his disk: it was gone. Niki had beaten him after all.

Niki had told Amie in a mind link that she was dead. It was best that way. She didn't want anyone to know she was a hawk. They'd worry, especially Amie. Maybe someday she would find her way back to human form but until then she would enjoy life from up here.

She flew toward the battlefield to see how they were doing.

Amie cringed but said nothing as tears flowed. Amie

gathered her strength and swallowed hard then stood tall and straight. She received Niki's message but would not think of it. Amie would have to put it out of her mind; she had to let it go.

"I'm going to construct a bridge far from the other. We'll lose too many lives fighting for that one," said Amie.

Jensen watched as directly before her stones rose one by one and shaped a bridge across the river. Stones and rocks came out of the bowels of the earth and flew into place next to each other. Jensen could see why Amie was known as the Legend of Tyhton. The bridge grew rapidly block by block.

Soldiers groaned in awe and looked toward the sorceress hands outstretched commanding the bridge to exist. It did.

Corel, magic sword in hand was the first to cross at the head of his troops. In full armour with his face shield down he was a sight to behold. The knight sat upon a large grey stallion and was known throughout the land in battledress as he had a large "C" imprinted on his armour.

On the other side Kago commander of the wizard's troops rode toward him.

"I will deal with the archers," said Amie.

Amie raised her arms causing a dense fog to cover archers positioned left and right of the battlefield.

Jensen rode over the bridge with Katie not far behind and Shaun close to her.

Kago dismounted and stood before Corel sword in hand, waiting. In answer Corel dismounted and the two fought.

"Stay beside me Katie, you too Shaun the wizard won't

dare fire near me. Hitting me would give me more strength, the last thing he needs," said Jensen.

Jensen watched the two commanders battle, their swords ringing throughout the valley. Corel landed a solid blow to Kago's arm then followed with a strike through the arm hole in his armour. Kago fell to his side but soon regained his footing, not hurt at all. Protected by magic he would heal as soon as he was cut. The sword did nothing for Corel as Jensen had thought. Corel was a better swordsman but would not beat him this day or any other.

Kago countered Corel's blows with a flurry of his own, backing him and knocking him to the ground. Kago drove his sword below the chest plate of Corel's armour and up. Corel lay dead and moved no more; the better man defeated by magic.

Kago backed toward his troops raising his sword in the air. Cheers came from his soldiers and the closest patted him on the back, one even tossed him a flask of ale.

Katie screamed driving her horse forward toward the body of Corel. Jensen called for her to return but to no avail; she raced toward the knight. A lightning bolt like a giant spear struck her sending her to the ground. Katie lay like a broken doll, her chest ruby red.

Jensen burst into tears; the battle had just started and was already lost. All of Corel's soldiers stood not knowing what to do, no one taking charge. None wanted to do battle against a man that could not be killed. No one wanted to be next to die.

Tears in her eyes Jensen walked her horse slowly toward Katie, fearing her friend was dead. Jensen dismounted and walked toward her best friend lying on the ground, hands in fists by her side. Part of her wanted to turn and run away and part of her had to know. With a scream Jensen hugged Katie's lifeless body and cried into her robe.

Shaun was kneeling beside Katie, tears pouring from him as well.

Jensen stood and faced the enemy not far from her. She saw Shaun walking toward Corel's body, Kago standing near. Shaun picked up the Sword of Kavar; the blade shone blue as it did for her; the sword accepted him as well.

Jensen walked closer to Shaun and saw his sword hand shake, his body trembled.

Then with a mighty scream of rage he lashed at Kago with hate in every stroke. His sword was not that of a master like Corel but his strokes were filled with determination leaving no doubt that either he or Kago would die. Shaun looked for weakness and found it knocking the sword from Kago's hand. Shaun drove the blade through Kago's armour as though it was made of paper. A sword through his heart Kago fell. With a mighty pull Shaun yanked the sword from Kago's chest. All waited for the dead man to rise. Silence filled the valley for an eternity: a horse whinnied, a raven overhead squawked, there was a slight tinkling of iron and still Kago lay silent.

Finally a man behind Shaun raised his sword and screamed in triumph then the whole valley was filled with a roar. Soldiers regained their courage and poured over the bridge to stand behind Shaun. The man who had slain a demon would now lead them into war.

Jensen walked to Shaun and touched his hand with new respect for him in her heart. She knew then that the knight she sought was with her from the very start.

Jensen boldly walked toward the enemy with the new first knight at her side. A serpent captain ran toward her sword above his head. Jensen stared into his eyes and commanded him to attack his own men which he did. In defence they had to strike the man down.

The army parted before her; anyone coming her way went mad and attacked the soldiers on his own side. A Koto-Ri warrior rushed toward Jensen and Shaun engaged. He struck with a rage shattering the Koto-Ri's sword with one blow then cutting her down with the next.

Killing Katie was to be the biggest mistake the Wizard had made today. Jensen looked into the eyes of the soldiers and thought of Katie. They moved further and further away.

Jensen heard a voice in her head; it was Presela.

"Kamahl is in the tent directly ahead, I sense your family is also near. Take care I also feel another with a gift but know not who."

Everyone looked west as horns sounded in the distance. Jensen stared at the hill where it all began for her; the hills where she stood and watched the soldiers invade their land. More horns sounded as the horizon filled with thousands of dwarfs. Two shadows like those of great eagles crossed the battlefield causing all to look high in the air; it was Sophie and Darrow.

Jensen looked at Katie's body once more then to the soldiers who stood in her way. Kamahl was like a plague in her life destroying or infecting all she held dear.

Jensen had enough; it was his time to die.

Jensen slowly walked toward thousands of soldiers with a threatening look in her eyes daring them to get in her way. Shaun and some knights gathered around protecting her from direct harm. Tension hung thick in the air.

"I only want Kamahl," yelled Jensen.

No one afterwards could explain what happened next. Someone said a man dropped a sword another said a soldier coughed. Each side said the other was to blame.

The soldiers behind Jensen burst into battle. Screams and threats worked their way through the battlefield and soon all engaged. The sound of iron and men filled the air. Shaun rallied more soldiers around Jensen and they slowly fought their way to the tent.

Thousands of dwarfs ran down the hill joining the battle below. The dwarfs with their war axes fought in teams of two; one cut low then the other cut high, a fighting style Kamahl's serpent warriors were not accustomed to. They fell like hay at the cut of a scythe.

From above flames from dragon's mouths burned into serpent soldiers melting armour and chain mail as they passed by. Shaun and Jensen were held at bay and almost overrun then Sophie dropped from the sky. Giant claws and dagger teeth slashed at the troops; Darrow landed beside his mate and ripped into soldiers as well. The dragons cleared a way to the wizard's tent and the fighting slowed. Jensen turned and looked back at the battlefield.

"It's between me and Kamahl," she yelled.

Word spread from mouth to another's ear and slowly the fighting stopped as they all gazed toward the tent. They were all spectators in the upcoming duel.

Jensen stared at a tent, unprotected by troops as the few guards left moved out of the way. She could feel the wizard within. Jensen entered the tent and saw the man in her nightmare, his skin the grey colour of death. It would feel good to touch him, to watch him crumble to dust. Kamahl avoided direct eye contact with her not wishing to be a victim of her gift. If Jensen could only get a look into those eyes she would make him kill himself.

"If you touch me you will never see your parents again," said the wizard.

Jensen looked at the man as she tried to slip a glance into his steel grey eyes. Had he won after all?

"I visited you in your dream, remember? I know who your parents are and also your two brothers. I have your parents and your brothers," said the wizard.

Jensen couldn't walk away and she knew it. If she left her family to him he would forever use them against her. Sooner or later it would come back to this. It might as well be now.

"If you take your soldiers and leave then I'll spare you, otherwise you will die here and now," said Jensen.

The wizard stared at the floor in indecision. She'd left him one of two choices; live or die. Then a slight smile broke on his face and looked up but not at her in an almost friendly manner.

"I anticipated your desire to reunite with your family so had them brought here. Now take them and leave and so shall I," said the wizard then waved to a guard outside.

Jensen watched her parents and her brothers walk into the tent. Jensen wanted to hug them but would show no weakness here. She pointed for them to exit, her eyes glued to the wizard.

Jensen wanted to kill the wizard more than anything in her life but had vowed to let him be in exchange for the lives of her family. Kenji told her that it was the purity within that made her gift work as it did. Breaking a vow would discredit her not only to the Gods that gave her the power but most of all to herself. Jensen had to walk away from a task half done.

Just as Jensen was about to leave a tall woman with blonde hair dressed in white appeared from nowhere to stand behind Kamahl. It was Ises. She had a dagger in hand and wore a smile. Kamahl had a look in his eyes as though he could feel her and started to turn. Kamahl was no fool; he was a wizard after all. Jensen had to choose between Kamahl and Ises. It was not a hard choice to make.

"Kamahl," shouted Jensen to get his attention.

Instead of turning to see what was coming his way he looked at Jensen.

Ises plunged the dagger deep into his back.

Kamahl groaned and dropped slowly to the floor. His body burned and decayed at an enormous rate. It turned to dust before everyone's eyes. That was all. The wizard was gone.

Jensen shook her head and knew justice had been done. The Gods had seen her plight as just.

Ises walked toward Jensen and smiled.

"Hello Jensen. I'm taking command of Kamahl's troops."

The commander Jensen had ordered to obey Ises on the Isle of the Gods was at her side holding her arm in his. Together they left the tent and walked toward their troops.

Jensen walked at the head of her family as the enemy troops nervously moved out of her way. Shaun was still at her side guarding her every step, blue sword in hand.

Ises holding the dagger and the commander's hand was not far behind.

"Kamahl is dead. I'm your new Queen. We will all leave this place," shouted Ises and then added loudly, "For now."

Jensen stopped and turned staring into the eyes of the priestess. There was a smile on Ises' face, the smile of a snake.

Had Jensen made the right choice? A dead tyrant and another quickly took his place. It was done; it was all over for now. Jensen had done what she set out to do; not many do in this life. Her family was free and well, so be it. Ises would rule in place of Kamahl.

Jensen took Biscuit's reins and walked to the other side of the bridge. The invading army was already dismantling tents and loading supplies preparing to leave. Jensen saw Amie, tears flowing from her eyes.

"What's wrong Amie?"

"Niki's dead."

"How, how do you know?"

"Niki told me. We can communicate mind to mind. She had to use all her power to block the pass. The wizard dealt her a fatal blow while she was weak. Niki told me she was dying and I know she is. I can feel her no more. Niki was like a daughter to me."

Jensen held Amie as she cried; it was a day for tears. They had lost much today and what had they achieved? Nothing if Ises was the same as the wizard.

Jensen tuned to her mother and hugged her tighter than she ever had before; her father was next and yes her pestering brothers as well. Amie in the lead they made their way back to the palace where the Taggart family was given rooms normally afforded only to persons of nobility.

The screech of a hawk sounded above; the bird dove toward them and soared close over their heads.

"It looks like we have a friend in the heavens," said Jensen.

Amie looked to the skies with that knowing all smile on her face.

Amie felt Niki again. She felt her in the hawk. For some reason Niki wanted all to think she was dead so Amie would honour that. Her heart warmed knowing how Niki had escaped Kamahl's wrath. Amie would have to find a way to bring her friend back.

"Yes. Yes we do."

Jensen waited for more and when nothing else came wondered what she knew that no one else did. Amie was like that; kept things to herself for some reason at times.

There was a celebration that evening on the palace grounds; a feast of a magnitude not ever seen in the land. After all there were dwarfs, and dragons to feed and no one knew who ate more.

Sides of beef were skewed and rotated above fire pits the night long. When one was finished another took its place, an endless line of meat roasted scenting the night air.

Hand shakes and laughter were the norm and not a cross word was exchanged. Sophie and Darrow were accepted by all for their part in the battle earlier that day. Old grievances were forgotten and new friends made as comrades of war basked in the glory of their victory.

Customs were shared between dwarfs, and men, dances and stories as well. Beautiful voices echoed tunes through the night and bards told tales as children sat slack jawed.

The wizard was dead and all rejoiced. In this world folk celebrated birth, life, and death as well. The demise of one tyrant meant life for many. It was a worthy trade but costly to attain as justice often is.

Morning came to Siscerly with the warm rays of the sun.

Birds scattered and horses jumped as two dragons took to the air. Sophie and Darrow were on the way home, their debt to the villagers paid.

The dwarfs were leaving after a hearty breakfast of sausage and ale. With Nikita gone talks of trade died with her as well. Amie said they would resume and ambassadors were exchanged.

Amie's soldiers had not been able to find the remains of the princess; only her clothing and gleaming in the sun her four rings.

Jensen mind was abuzz; the wizard was dead and her family free. It couldn't get any better than this. Then like a thud in her heart she remembered Katie and her spirits sank. Would things always be this way? Jensen felt empty within; she missed Katie. She needed to see Kenji.

# THE GIFTED OF SISCERLY XXXIII
## *The lost Soul*

JENSEN RODE BISCUIT TOWARD Sharks Way stopping at the field where she had found Shaun. No wizard waited here for her today; the man was finally dead. Jensen took the mare to the stable upon reaching town and ran to Katie's cabin. She pushed the broken door open and slowly stepped inside in her heart hoping to see Katie standing by the hearth. Katie would tell her that some unknown magic had saved her and all would be back to the way it was before. No one stood by the hearth or anywhere inside. Jensen ambled around the cabin looking closer at things she had seen before. No one had taken advantage of the open door and robbed her but then Katie was a witch; no sane person would steal from a witch.

Jensen ran her hands across Katie's things; her friend had few possessions but shared what little she had. Jensen lay on the bed gazing at the wooden roof. Katie was welcome at the castle; all were her friends. So why stay here in an old cabin? She had to see Kenji and find out more.

Jensen rode toward the wall of mist, a gateway to the

Underworld. If one walked into the fog left or right of the swamp they would be forever lost amongst the dead. Their souls would belong to the Keeper and given to the ravaging spirits that had earned their way to power in this dark kingdom. Kamahl would now be one.

Life was the same way on both sides of the mist; existence of any kind absent within the stagnant swamp. Grey dead trees stood like waiting ghosts under an iron sky. Jensen remembered Katie's struggle with the monster snake and smiled thinking about the strength she'd shown. Biscuit was nervous every step of the way and glad to break through the fog on the other side. Nothing challenged them this time as before.

The mountains lay before her unseen until beyond the hazy sky. On this side the sun shone and the birds sang; the forests were teeming with life. Jensen followed the trail, deer bouncing around through the high grass unsure of her intent. She searched the skies above for signs of ill will but saw only hawks circling the heavens.

The sun was slowly giving way to the moon as Jensen came upon stones set in a circle. The remains of a campfire she had made when Katie and her passed not that long ago. Jensen unsaddled Biscuit and let the mare graze. She gathered firewood for the night. Wolves howled in the distance, her little mare edging closer to the campfire with every call.

Jensen did not know that the loss of a friend could cause such emptiness within but then Katie was more than a friend. She was a mentor who guided her soul through life. Without her Jensen would be long dead. Jensen sat near the fire thinking of Katie sometimes crying and sometimes breaking into a laugh. The sun caught her still awake and throwing another log onto the fire. Biscuit lay asleep in the grass not far from her. The little mare trusted her to keep the wolves at bay while she slept.

Jensen woke Biscuit and threw some sand on the fire. The grass was lush and would probably not burn but Katie always insisted she extinguish the flames when breaking camp, even when in a swamp. Jensen followed the trail high into the mountains watching the eagles soar. For what remained of her life she would search the heavens for signs of the wizard; his orange disk in the sky would be forever burned in her mind. Jensen was between the two mountains where her body would lay today if not for Kenji. She knew Kenji was close and aware of her coming.

Biscuit tiptoed her way up the mountain side snorting every now and then as the going was not an easy task. Jensen held her hand up toward the rock as Katie had done before. An opening into the cavern appeared before her; she was welcome. Jensen walked her horse into the far end of the cave and dismounted. She put her mount in the pen and tossed her some hay. Jensen filled a pail with water then set it down before Biscuit.

Jensen followed the tunnels and soon found why Katie had not lost her way. At every intersection requiring a decision of direction the way was known to her; Jensen knew without doubt the path she must take. Kenji had told her that if she was welcome the way would be known to her. She stood at the doorway where Katie had halted and did so not knowing why. A tiny voice soon whispered in her ear.

"Please come in."

Jensen entered and saw Kenji at the far end of the cavern. Without looking about she walked toward the woman, unable to hold back the flood of tears. Jensen threw her arms around

Kenji and wept. Feeling tears on her skin she looked at Kenji, her eyes swollen as hers.

"Katie is dead," said Jensen.

"I know child, oh how I know."

They both hugged and wept.

"Let's sit and talk," said Kenji.

Kenji led her to her favourite room, the kitchen.

"I miss her so," sobbed Jensen.

"So do I. She was my daughter you know."

"No, she never told me."

"She never knew."

"She didn't look like you."

"Oh yes she looked exactly like me, dark hair, light skin. It was as though I gazed upon myself in a mirror."

"She had red hair and blue eyes," said Jensen.

"That was the body of another with her mind inside."

"What?"

"Her own body was tortured to death by a wizard trying to find a way to conquer me. He kept her mind and soul alive to feel the fire of what he did to her," said Kenji.

"How did she become who she was?"

"He left her on the face of this mountain for me to find. I could not let her soul die. I found a woman whose mind was lost and her body dying for lack of direction so implanted Katie's soul and spirit into the woman. Both were saved.

"But I did break a law of nature that I had always lived by in doing so. For that the Gods imprisoned me in this mountain. If I leave I'm no longer mortal and will die. It is punishment for tampering with fate. I'd do it again in a minute for her," said Kenji.

"How could she not know you, how could she not know what had happened?"

"I erased her mind of her previous life. It was as though she was reborn. Katie was such a good soul, pure and devoid of all evil. She would never have allowed me to save her the way I did. She would never rob another of even a second of life."

"Can you do it again?"

"Oh child, I can't find her soul, it's lost to me. I try so hard but cannot find it. I think the Gods are hiding it from me."

Both talked endlessly as time passed, days and days. Kenji walked to a tapestry of a castle. She waved her hand before it and the castle at Siscerly animated before them. Miniature men and horses moved before them exactly as if they were standing in a high building looking down at the square. The land was in disorder, people running to and fro, in all directions.

"You must return Jensen, Tyhton needs you," said Kenji.

Jensen wanted to stay with Kenji if not forever then at least for a time. Kenji had so much of Katie to share it was as though she were yet alive. She hugged Kenji once more then reluctantly left. Jensen saddled Biscuit and set out for the castle not knowing what possible help she could be.

# The Gifted of Siscerly XXXIV
## *The New Princess*

Jensen left the mountain stronghold and rode back the way she came. A lonely ride for a day and a half took her back to Sharks Way. She took Biscuit to the stable then went to the inn for something to eat. Men were talking of the chaos within Tyhton. The Princess was dead and left no heir. Ambitious relatives were claiming the throne. Two cousins and a niece argued amongst themselves and were assembling forces; a civil war would result. Jensen listened while she ate but felt it was all out of her hands; she was just a peasant girl from Cambells Cross.

Jensen left the inn and once more returned to Katie's cabin. She slept in Katie's bed hugging her blanket. Morning came too soon, the sunlight piercing through the windows hurt her eyes. She rose then wandered to the inn for breakfast. Some men were still talking as though they were deciding the fate of the kingdom. Jensen paid little attention as she nibbled at her food, her mind focused on the past.

Biscuit raced through the castle gates unobstructed by

guards as horse and rider were known throughout the land. They quickly slowed as people walking to and fro crowded the street. Most carried food or possessions as though preparing for a siege. Soldiers on horseback pushed their way through then hurried out the front gate.

Jensen took Biscuit to the stables and tended to her as no stable hands were to be found. Few horses remained; the place looked abandoned. She went to the Palace which was also in disarray. Officials ran up and down the stairs, in and out of doors the length of the hall. An army captain swore to himself as he walked out the palace door.

Jensen made her way up the stairs dodging others as she went. She had finally made it to Niki's old stateroom and found the waiting area crowded. No room to sit she stood waiting her turn. Jensen wanted to see if Amie needed her help. People walked in and out of the waiting room seeming to fill faster than it emptied. Jensen felt uneasy as the others stared at her then whispered to each other while looking her way.

An aid to Amie was escorting a man out the door when she saw Jensen.

"Oh no, come in, we've had soldiers searching for you, where have you been?" said the aid.

Jensen walked in the door and upon seeing her Amie rushed her way.

"Oh, how are you?"

"I'm fine, is there anything I can do to help?" asked Jensen.

"These are serious times. The country is on the brink of civil war but I won't let that happen. In the absence of a monarch I am Keeper of the Realm and I ask your help to lead this country," said Amie.

"Me? How? Why?"

"You are the one who put an end to the wizard. The people love and respect you. They need a strong leader and there is no one they would accept other than you. As Keeper of the Realm I declare you our leader by merit of what you have done for us. You can rule as a Princess."

"I can't do it, I'm a peasant girl not a princess," said Jensen.

"Nonsense child. You have wisdom beyond your years, courage, and a kind heart. I make you our leader in any case. You can refuse to rule of course but I certainly hope you will. I will stand at your side," said Amie.

"Would that not hasten a civil war?"

"Who would dare oppose an army led by you with Shaun at your side? Besides that the people would never oppose you."

Jensen stood trembling needing Katie's council more than ever. She looked into Amie's eyes and saw despair and need.

"I'll do it for you if you think it will help."

"I'll make ready the preparations. You will be crowned tomorrow midday."

The last part of the day Jensen spent being attended to by fitters. They were led by a man who glared at her up and down; they measured her, poked and prodded. She hoped the result was worth the work. All this fuss over a peasant girl from Cambells Cross she thought.

Jensen could not sleep, she tossed and turned then finally gave into the notion that tired as she was would spend the night awake. Jensen dressed and walked down to the kitchen where she sampled food in shelves and bowls set upon the counter tops. Jensen sat, laid her head on her arm and fell asleep.

Daylight surprised her as the kitchen staff scolded her for sleeping on the table unaware she was the one they were rushing for. Jensen returned to her room filled with servants waiting to prepare her for the day ahead. She was bathed, had her hair brushed and was dressed by others; second time since she was four.

Jensen walked out of the castle door wearing a white dress which stretched to the ground. Amie waited, smiling, a crown in her hands. It was made of gold, the front high tapering to a band in the rear. The front was etched and filled with rubies, emeralds, and sapphires. Amie placed the crown upon her head as thousands cheered.

One hundred mounted lancers lined the street double file. Biscuit was led to the front of the procession. Jensen smiled at her parents and brothers, beaming with pride. She walked toward Biscuit and mounted amidst cheers. Shaun her first Knight rode to her right side. Together followed by the lancers they rode through the streets where they were showered in flowers. Jensen Taggart sixteen years old, the Princess of Tyhton; what are the folks at Cambells Cross thinking of now. The little redhead they shunned for being a witch. Well they were right in that at least.

Niki clutched the branch of an oak tree and watched the procession. She knew that little woman could turn the tide of battle and win the hearts and support of all. Jensen would make an excellent princess and look after everyone. For the first time in her life Niki felt free; free from the responsibility of royalty she'd had since birth. Niki took flight and went wherever she wanted to go.

Jensen wanted to sleep after the long hard day but felt obligated to attend the dinner held in her honour. She would have to get used to days like these and saw many in her future. Representatives from all walks of life greeted her and wished her well.

The coming weeks passed quickly as Jensen moved about the countryside in an effort to rebuild a war stricken land. She ordered that all victims of war be brought to the castle. Inside the walls they could at least camp in safety. The large fountain provided water and food was brought in daily from surrounding farms. All was funded by Jensen's dwindling treasury. Complaints by shopkeepers of thieves in the streets poured in daily but few accusations proved to be true. Jensen was thankful that Amie's diplomacy kept all in order and under control.

Lonely, Jensen would wander the streets in the evening looking upon the ones she was trying to help. This night she watched as a woman lit a campfire by passing her hands over the branches the way Katie used to do. Jensen looked upon the woman's golden hair, a dried patch of blood at the back of her head. When she turned her way Jensen looked into sunken blue eyes surrounded by black rings. Beauty had been used for something never intended. The woman had been badly beaten by someone for reasons unknown. It was the times, the way things were after a war. Jensen started to walk away when the woman spoke.

"You wouldn't have the price of an ale would you?"

"Hah, yes, oh yes I have. What's your name?" asked Jensen.

"I don't know? Come to think of it I don't know much of anything."

"Well, how does Katie sound?"

"Familiar."

"Thanks Kenji."

"Come and visit," the sound was whispered only into her ear.

"Sooner than you think," said Jensen.

"Whose Kenji?" asked Katie.

"Oh, you'll meet her soon."

"Look at that handsome guy," said Katie.

"You know I need and adviser. What are you doing for the next fifty years?"

## THE END